"WHO ARE THESE PEOPLE? WHAT DO THEY WANT FROM US?"

It was, Han Solo thought, a reasonable question Badure was asking the droid Bollux. Their party had stumbled across what looked like a used-spaceship lot, then discovered that all the craft on display were crude mockups—and then been captured by men speaking a long-forgotten language and imprisoned deep beneath the planet's surface. There were, it seemed, a lot of things that needed explaining . . . but Bollux, who had established a queer kind of rapport with their captors, didn't seem too happy with the answers he had come up with.

Sounding dismayed, the droid said slowly, "I know it sounds absurd in this day and age, sir, but unless we can do something, you're all about to become, er, a human sacrifice."

HAN SOLO AND THE LOST LEGACY

From the Adventures of
Luke Skywalker

by Brian Daley

Based on the characters and
situations created by
George Lucas

A DEL REY BOOK

BALLANTINE BOOKS • NEW YORK

A book for Linda Kuehl
and, with particular gratitude,
for John A. Kearney

A Del Rey Book
Published by Ballantine Books

Library of Congress Catalog Card Number: 80-66168

ISBN 0-345-28710-X

Printed in Canada

First Edition: September 1980
Fifth Printing: October 1980

First Canadian Printing: September 1980
Fourth Canadian Printing: September 1981

Covert art by William Schmidt

☐ I

HAN Solo nearly had the control-stem leads hooked up, a sweaty job that had him stuck under the low-slung airspeeder for almost an hour, when there was a kick at his foot. "What's holding things up?"

The leads, now gathered together in precise order, sprang free of his fingers, going every which way. With a scalding Corellian malediction, Han shoved against the machine's undercarriage, and his repulsor-lift mechanic's creeper slid out from under the airspeeder.

Han leaped up instantly to confront Grigmin, his temporary employer, the color on his face changing from the red of frustration to a darker and more dangerous hue. Han was lean, of medium height, and appeared younger than his actual age. His eyes were guarded, intense.

Grigmin, tall, broad shouldered, handsomely blond, and some years younger than Han, either didn't notice his pit-crewman's anger or chose not to acknowledge it. "Well? What about it? That airspeeder's an important part of my show."

Han attempted not to lose his scant temper. Working as pit-crewman to Grigmin's one-man airshow on a circuit of fifth-rate worlds had been the only job he and his partner, Chewbacca, had been able to get when they found they needed work, but Grigmin's unrelenting arrogance made the task of keeping his outmoded aircraft running nearly unbearable.

"Grigmin," Han said, "I've warned you before. You put too much strain on your hardware. You could stay well within performance tolerances and still complete every maneuver in your routines. But instead you showboat, with junk heaps that were obsolete when the Clone Wars were news."

Grigmin's grin grew even wider. "Save the excuses, Solo. Will my airspeeder be ready for my afternoon show, or have you and your Wookiee sidekick decided you don't like working for me?"

Masterpiece of understatement! Han thought to himself, but mumbled, "She'll be in the air again if Fadoop gets here with the replacement parts."

Now Grigmin frowned. "You should have gone for them yourself. I never trust these useless locals; it's a rule I have."

"If you want me to use a starship for a crummy surface-to-surface skip, you'll have to pay the expenses—up front." Han would sooner trust a local like the amiable, gregarious Fadoop than a shifty deadbeat like Grigmin.

Grigmin ignored the invitation to part with some cash. "I want my airspeeder ready," he concluded and left to prepare for the next part of his performance, an exhibition of maneuvers with a one-man jetpack. *Maneuvers any academy greenie could do,* Han thought. *These backwater worlds are the only place anyone would pay to see a feeble act like Grigmin's.*

Still, if it hadn't been for Grigmin's needing a pit-crew, Han Solo and the Wookiee, Chewbacca, free-lance smugglers, would have been on the Hurt Vector. He adjusted his sweatband, toed the mechanic's creeper over to him, settled onto it, and pulled himself back under the airspeeder.

Groping half-heartedly for the control leads, Han wondered just what it was that made his luck so erratic. He had had strokes of good fortune that rivaled anything he had ever heard of, but at other times. . . .

He barked his knuckles, swore a mighty oath, and mulled over the fact that only a short time ago he and his Wookiee partner had held the galaxy by the tail. They had defied a slavery ring in the Corporate Sector, held the Authority's dreaded Security Police at bay with a Territorial Manager as hostage, and come out of the deal ten thousand credits richer.

But since then there had been needed repairs for their starship, the *Millennium Falcon,* and monumental celebrations on a dozen worlds as they put the Corporate Sector behind them. Then there had been ill-fated smuggling ventures: a ruinous try at clotheslegging in the Cron Drift; a failed Military Script–exchange plot in the Lesser Plooriod Cluster; and more, each adventure bringing a little closer that day when they would find themselves among the needy.

So they had ended up here in the Tion Hegemony, so far out among the lesser star systems of the vast Empire that the Imperials didn't even bother to exert direct control over it. In the Tion tended to congregate the petty grifters, unsuccessful con-artists, and unprosperous crooks of the galaxy. They ran *Chak*-root, picked up R'alla mineral water for the smuggling run to Rampa, swiped, ambushed, connived, and attempted in a thousand ways to fuel careers temporarily at a standstill.

Han considered all this as he carefully gathered the leads, once again separating them delicately. At least with Grigmin, Han and Chewbacca were paid, once in a while.

But that didn't make it any easier to take Grigmin's high-handedness. What particularly irritated Han was that Grigmin considered himself the hottest stunt pilot in space. Han had entertained the idea of taking a swing at the younger man, but Grigmin was a former heavyweight unarmed-combat champion. . . .

His musings were interrupted by another kick that jolted his boot. The control leads sprang from his hands again. Furious, he pushed off against the airspeeder's undercarriage, jumped off the mechanic's creeper, and, combat champion or no, launched himself at his tormentor . . .

. . . and was caught up instantly against a wide shaggy chest in a frightfully strong but restrained hug and held a half-meter or so off the ground.

"Chewie! Let go, you big . . . all right; I'm sorry."

Thick arms muscled like loops of steel released him. The Wookiee Chewbacca glared down from his towering height, growling a denunciation of Han's manners, his reddish-brown brows lowered, his fangs showing. He shook a long, hairy finger at his partner for emphasis and tried straightening the Authority Security Police admiral's hat perched rakishly on his head, his lush mane escaping from beneath it.

The admiral's hat was just about the only thing the two still had from their adventures in the Corporate Sector. Chewbacca had taken a fancy to its bright braid, snowy-white material, glossy black brim, and ornate insignia during an exchange of hostages just before their hasty departure from that region of space. In his people's tradition of counting coup on their enemies, the Wookiee had demanded the hat as part of the ransom. Han, pressed by events, had indulged him.

Now the pilot threw up his hands. "Enough! I *said* I was sorry. I thought you were that vapor-brain Grigmin again. Now what?"

Han's giant copilot informed him that Fadoop had arrived. Fadoop stood nearby on her feet and knuckles, an unusually fat and outgoing native of the planet Saheelindeel. A short, bandy-legged, and densely green-furred primate, she was a local wheeler-dealer who flew an aircraft of sorts, an informal assemblage of parts and components from various scrapped fliers, a craft which she called *Skybarge*.

Pulling off his sweatband, Han walked toward Fadoop. "You scrounged the parts? Good gal!"

Fadoop, scratching behind one ear with a big toe, removed a malodorous black cigar from her mouth and blew a smoke ring. "Anything for Solo-my-friend. Are we not soulsealed buddies, you, me, and the Big One here, this Wookiee? But, ahh, there is a matter—"

Fadoop looked away somewhat embarrassed. Working the quid of *Chak*-root that swelled her cheek, she spat a stream of red liquid into the dust. "I trust Solo-my-friend, but not Grigmin-the-blowhard. I hate to bring up money."

"No apologies; you earned it." Han dug into a coverall pocket for the cash he had gotten in advance for the airspeeder parts. Fadoop tucked the money away swiftly into her belly pouch, then brightened; a twinkle sparkled in her close-set, golden eyes.

"And there's a surprise, Solo-my-friend. At the spaceport, when I picked up the parts, two new arrivals were looking for you and the Big One. I had room in my ship, and so brought them with me. They wait."

Han reached back under the airspeeder and drew out his coiled gunbelt, which he always kept at arm's length. "Who are they? Imperials? Did they look like skip-tracers or Guild muscle?" He buckled the custom-model blaster around his hips, fastening the tiedown at his right thigh, and snapped open his holster's retaining strap.

Fadoop objected. "Negatron! Nice, peaceful fellows, a little nervous." She scratched her verdant, bulging midsection, making a sandpaper sound. "They want to hire you. No weapons on them, at least."

That sounded reassuring. "What do you think?" Han asked Chewbacca.

The Wookiee resettled his admiral's cap, pulling the gleaming brim down low over his eyes, and stared across the airfield. After a few seconds, he barked a syllable of affirmation, and the three started off for Fadoop's ship.

It was high festival on Saheelindeel, formerly a time of tribal reunions and hunting rituals, then of fertility and harvest ceremonies. Now it incorporated elements of an airshow and industrial fair. Saheelindeel, like so many other planets in the Tion Hegemony, was struggling to thrust itself into an age of modern technology and prosperity in emulation of the galaxy at large. Farming machinery was on display as well as factory robotry. Vehicles new to the wide-eyed Saheelindeeli but obsolete on more advanced worlds were in evidence, along with communications and holo apparatuses that delighted the touring crowd. In an exhibition game of shock-ball, the charged orb sizzled between players wearing insulated mitts; the winning team was using a zoned offense.

Off in the distance, Grigmin was looping and diving

in jetpack harness. Just seeing him again put Han in a more receptive frame of mind to meet Fadoop's passengers. Passing by the reviewing stand, he saw the Saheelindeeli's grizzled matriarch holding the elaborate trophy she was to present that afternoon for the best thematic float or exhibit. The fair's theme was *Fertility of the Soil, Challenge of the Sky*. Favored heavily to win was the opulent float entered by the Regional Fork-Pitchers' Local.

At last Han and his companions arrived at Fadoop's slapdash cargo ship. Despite her reassurances, Han was relieved to see the new arrivals were not Imperial stormtroopers—"snowmen" or "white-hats," as they were called in slangtalk—but an unassuming pair, human and humanoid.

The humanoid—a tall, reedy, purple-skinned type whose eyes, protruding from an elongated skull, held tiny red pinpoints of pupil—nodded at Han. "Ah, Captain Solo? A pleasure to meet you, sir!" He stuck out a thin arm. Han clasped the long, slender hand, trying to ignore its greasy skin secretions.

"Yes, I'm Solo. What can I do for you?"

The human, an emaciated albino wearing a sunproof robe, explained. "We represent the Committee for Interinstitutional Assistance of the University of Rudrig. You've heard of our school?"

"I think so." He vaguely remembered that it was the only decent advanced school in the Tion Hegemony.

"The university has concluded an Agreement of Aid for a fledgling college on Brigia," the albino continued.

The humanoid took up the conversation. "I am Hissal, and Brigia is my homeworld. The university has promised us guidance, materials, and teaching aids."

"So you should be contacting Tion Starfreight or Interstellar Shipping," Han noted. "But you came looking for us. Why?"

"The shipment is completely legal," the gaunt Hissal hastened to add, "but there is opposition from my planetary government. Though they can't contravene

Imperial trade agreements, of course, we still fear there might be trouble in making delivery and—"

"—you want someone who can look out for your stuff."

"Your name *had* come to us as a capable fellow's," Hissal admitted.

"Chewie and I try to avoid trouble—"

"The job pays rather well," interposed the albino. "One thousand credits."

"—unless there's some profit in it. Two thousand," Han finished, doubling the price automatically even though the offer had been more than fair. There ensued a few moments of haggling. But when Han pressed the university representatives too sharply and their enthusiasm began to waver, Chewbacca issued a howl that made them all jump. He didn't much like crewing for Grigmin either.

"Uh, my copilot's an idealist," Han improvised, scowling up at the Wookiee. "Luckily for you. Fifteen hundred." The albino and the Brigian agreed, adding that half would be paid on consignment, half on delivery. Chewbacca pushed his gaudy admiral's hat back on his head and beamed at his partner, overjoyed to be lifting off again.

"So," said Fadoop, slapping her belly merrily with both hands and one foot, "that only leaves telling that fool Grigmin good riddance."

"It does, doesn't it?" Han agreed. "He'll be doing his big stunt display any time now." He rubbed his jaw and studied the ungainly, stubby-winged vessel that stood nearby. "Fadoop, can I borrow old *Skybarge* for a few minutes?"

"No questions asked. But she's got cargo onboard, several cubic meters of enriched fertilizer for the agricultural pavilion." Fadoop relit her cigar.

"No problem," Han told her. "Warm up your ship. I'll be right back."

Having already amazed the unsophisticated Saheelindeeli with his hover-sled, jetpack, and repulsorlift swoops, Grigmin began his grand finale, an exhibition of stunt flying with an obsolete X-222 high-altitude fighter. The triple-deuce looped, climbed, dove, and banked through textbook maneuvers, releasing clouds of colorful aerosols at certain points to the delight of the crowd.

Grigmin came into his final approach, putting the limber and lean ship through a fancy aerobatic display before coming in toward a precise landing. He didn't realize, however, that a second ship had come in after him on the same approach his fighter had taken. It was Fadoop's cumbersome *Skybarge* with Han Solo at the controls. To show what he thought of Grigmin's flying ability, Han took the tubby ship through the same display the exhibition flier was just completing. But, coming into his first loop, Han feathered his portside engine.

The green-furred Saheelindeeli gasped collectively and pointed the second ship out to one another with a great commotion, forgetting to watch Grigmin's landing entirely. They expected to see *Skybarge* plummet from the air. But Han completed the roll, deftly working with the nearly empty craft's stubby wings, control surfaces, and chugging engine. On the second roll, he feathered the starboard engine, too, and went into a third with zero thrust.

Shrieks of fright from the crowd and their tentative race for cover abated as they saw that the unwieldy aircraft was still under control. Jumping up and down, pointing with fingers and toes, they sent up a ragged cheer for the mad pilot, then a more forceful one, reflecting the Saheelindeeli affection for grand gestures, even insane ones.

Grigmin, who had exited from his ship virtually unnoticed, threw down his flight helmet and watched *Skybarge* in mounting fury. Han coaxed the third roll out of his homely vessel and waggled her down toward the strip.

But only one landing wheel emerged from its bay. Grigmin grinned at the prospect of a crash; but unexpectedly the ship bounced off the single wheel, trimmed handily, and settled a second time as another landing wheel lowered. She bore on the reviewing stand with surprising grace and rebounded from two wheels.

As *Skybarge* neared the reviewing stand, the crowd parted before her, clapping their hands and feet in high approbation. The ship waggled her tail in midair, extended her third and last landing wheel, and rolled cleanly for the reviewing stand. By that time Grigmin was so distracted that he didn't notice the cargo ship heading directly for his precious triple-deuce fighter.

Too late! Slam! He could only dodge out of the way as *Skybarge* rolled by. Han threw a wicked grin at him from the cockpit.

Skybarge's high, heavy-duty landing gear permitted her to pass directly over the low, sleek fighter. With consummate skill, Han flipped open her cargo-bay doors and suddenly an avalanche of enriched fertilizer dumped directly into the fighter through the open cockpit canopy.

The Saheelindeeli began applauding madly. *Skybarge*'s overhead cockpit hatch popped open, and Han's happy face appeared. He inclined his head graciously to acknowledge the ovation as Grigmin was being elbowed farther and farther away by the press of the crowd.

From the reviewing stand the matriarch's voice wheezed through the crackling public address system. "First prize! Trophy to *Skybarge* for best exhibit, *Fertility of the Soil, Challenge of the Sky.*" She waved the tall loving cup as her advisers whistled and stomped their feet in glee.

☐ II

THE *Millennium Falcon* rested on Brigia's single spaceport landing field. She looked very much like the battered, much-repaired, and worn-out stock freighter she was, but there were incongruities. The irregular docking tackle, oversized thruster ports, heavy-weapons turrets, and late-model sensor-suite dish betrayed something about her real line of work.

"That's the last of the tapes," Han announced. He checked the offloading on his hand-held readout screen as Bollux, the labor droid, stumped past, guiding a repulsorlift hand truck. The automaton's green finish looked eerie in the glow of the irradiators with which the ship was now rigged. Brigia was flagged in all the standard directories, thus requiring phase-one decontam procedures. The ship's environmental systems circulated broad-spectrum anticontamination aerosols along with air. Han's and Chewbacca's immunization treatments would protect them against local maladies, but they were nonetheless eager to be away.

Han watched Bollux head for the steam-powered freight truck parked near the ship. The glare of the landing field's illumigrids showed him the Brigian workers, all volunteers from the budding college, arranging crates, packing canisters and carry-cases that the *Falcon* had delivered. They conversed animatedly among themselves, thrilled with the new broadcasting equipment and especially with the library of tapes.

Han turned to Hissal, who had accompanied him on the flight and who was to be the college's first president. "The only thing left to get outboard is your duplicator."

"Ah, yes, the duplicator, our most-awaited item,"

commented Hissal, "and the most expensive. It will print and collate material at speeds our own presses cannot match and synthesize any paper or other material from the raw constituents it contains. This, from a device that fits into a few crates. Amazing!"

Han made a noncommittal sound. Bollux was returning, and Han called down the curve of the passageway, "Chewie! Secure the main hold and crack open the number two; I want to get that duplicator off and raise ship." From aft echoed the Wookiee's answering growl.

"Captain, there's one more thing," Hissal went on, drawing a pouch from beneath his lateral folds. Han's right hand dropped immediately to his blaster. Hissal, sensing his breach of decorum, held up a thin hand in denial.

"Be of tranquil mind. I know that among your kind it is customary to offer a gratuity for a task well done." Hissal plucked a curl of bills out of his pouch and extended it to the pilot.

Han examined the bills. They had a strange texture, more like textile than like paper. "What *is* this stuff?"

"A new innovation," admitted Hissal. "Several Progressions ago the New Regime replaced bartering and local coinages with a planet-wide monetary system."

Han slapped the sheaf of minutely inscribed bills against the palm of his flying glove. "Which gives them a hammerlock on trade, of course. Well, thanks anyway, but this stuff isn't worth much off-planet."

Hissal's elongated face grew even longer. "Unfortunately, only the New Regime may hold off-world currency; thus, all equipment and materials for our school had to come by donation. The first thing the New Regime did when it accumulated enough credits was bring in a developmental consulting firm. Aside from the currency system, the firm's main accomplishment was to profit from a major purchase of military equipment, which included that warship you saw."

Han *had* noticed the ship, a pocket-cruiser of the outmoded Marauder class surrounded by worklights and armed guards.

"Her main control stacks blew on her shakedown

cruise," Hissal explained. "Naturally, there are no Brigian techs capable of repairing her, and so she remains inert until the Regime can muster enough credits to import techs and parts. That money could have brought us commercial technology, or medical advancements."

Han nodded. "First thing most of these boondock worlds do—no offense, Hissal—is pick up some toys to build their image. Then their neighbors run out and do the same."

"We are a poor planet," the Brigian told him solemnly, "and have more important priorities."

Han declined further comment on that subject. Bollux had returned and was waiting for Han's next order, when suddenly there was a distant screeching of steam sirens.

Han walked down to the ramp's hinged foot. Closing in from all sides were rows of lumbering metal power wagons, petro-engines chugging, sirens ripping the night, high wheels making the landing field tremble. Arc-spotlights swung to converge on the *Millennium Falcon* and the freight truck.

Han shouldered past Hissal and dashed to the ramp head. "Chewie! We've got problems; get into the cockpit and charge up the main guns!" He rejoined Hissal halfway down the ramp.

The college volunteers stood surprised and unmoving on the bed of their truck, unsure of what to do. In moments the cordon of power wagons had been drawn tightly. Doors flew open and squads of figures came leaping from the vehicles. They were obviously government troops, carrying old-fashioned solid-projectile firearms. But something about their uniforms seemed odd. The troops wore human-style military regalia ill-suited to the gawkish Brigian anatomy. Han surmised that remnants and leftovers had been foisted off on the unsuspecting New Regime as part of their overall military purchase.

The soldiers marched in badly fitting battle harness, far-too-loose helmets perched precariously on their heads, filigreed epaulets sagging forlornly from their narrow shoulders, embroidered dispatch cases flopping against their skinny posteriors. Their legs and feet were too narrow for combat boots, so the warriors of Brigia wore natty pink spats with glittering buttons over bare feet. Among what Han assumed to be their officer corps were an abundance of medals and citations, one or two ceremonial swords, and several drooping cummerbunds. A number of troopers with no detectable talent were blowing bugles.

In moments, the soldiers had taken the shocked college volunteers captive at bayonet point. Other units advanced on the starship.

Han had already grasped Hissal's thin arm and was dragging him up the ramp. "But, this is an atrocity! We have done nothing wrong!"

Han released him and plunged through the main hatch. "You want to debate that with a bullet? Make up your mind; I'm sealing up."

Hissal hurried up the ramp. The main hatch rolled down just as the troops reached the ramp's foot; Han heard a salvo of bullets ricocheting off it.

In the cockpit, Chewbacca had already activated defensive shields and had begun warming up the engines. Hissal, trailing Han, was still protesting. Han couldn't take the time to reply; he was completely absorbed in readying the ship for takeoff.

The volunteers were being dragged, pushed, and thrown into confinement in the waiting wagons. The few who protested were summarily struck down and towed off by their slender, strangely boned ankles. Han noticed that the Brigians' war-bannered personnel carriers were, in fact, garbage trucks of an outdated model.

Chewbacca made a grating sound through clenched teeth. "I'm mad about our money, too," Han replied. "How do we get the other half if we can't get a delivery receipt?"

The troops were taking up firing positions in ranks around the starship. "They couldn't have waited another ten minutes?" Han muttered. A Brigian stepped out in front of the firing lines. Because of the glare of the spotlights, Han had to shield his eyes with his hand to see that the Brigian held a loudhailer in one hand and an official-looking scroll in the other.

Han donned his headset and flipped on an external audio pickup in time to hear "—no harm will come to you, good friends from space! The peace-loving New Regime requires only that you surrender the fugitive now onboard your vessel. The Brigian government will trouble you no further."

Han keyed his headset mike over to external-speaker mode. "What about our pay?" He avoided looking at Hissal, but kept one hand close to his side arm.

"Agreements can be reached, honored offworlder," the Brigian below answered. "Allow me to come onboard and parlay."

Han keyed his mike again. "Pull the soldiers back and turn those spotlights off. Meet me at the ramp, no weapons, no stunts!"

The Brigian passed his loudhailer to a subordinate and motioned with the scroll. The ranks fell back and the spotlights flickered out; the martial garbage trucks withdrew. "Keep an eye on things," Han instructed his first mate. "If anyone moves wrong, let me know."

Hissal was outraged. "Is it your plan to treat with these hoodlums? Legally speaking, they haven't got a *crowbt* to stand on, I assure you. The courts—"

"—don't concern us now," Han interrupted, motioning him aside. "Go find a seat in the forward compartment and don't worry; we won't hand you over to them."

With great dignity Hissal corrected him. "My concern is for my friends."

Bollux, the labor droid, was waiting in the passageway, the crated duplicator components loaded on his handtruck. In his measured drawl the automaton asked, "What are your instructions, Captain?"

Han sighed. "I don't know. Why is it I never get the easy jobs? Go up forward, Bollux. If I need you, I'll holler." The machine's heavy feet clattered on the deckplates. Chewbacca yeowled that the area was clear.

Han pulled his blaster. The main hatch rolled up, and at the ramp's foot waited the Brigian. He was taller than Hissal, broadly built for his species, his color a little darker than average. He wore a chrome-studded battle harness, rhinestone shoulderboards with dangling brushes at the ends, several colorful aiguillettes, a salad of decorations, and impressive, red-sequined spats. A plume bobbed from his tilting helmet.

Han beckoned warily. The creature marched up the ramp, the scroll tucked under one arm. Han stopped him at the head of the ramp. "Shuck the harness and the tin lid and toss them back down."

The creature complied. "Welcome to our fair planet, fellow biped," he said with an effort at hearti-ness. "I am Inspector Keek, Chief of the Internal Se-curity Police of the very progress-minded New Regime of Brigia." He cast his harness and helmet away with a racket of clanking metal.

"I figured you weren't the Boosters' Club," Han said wryly, making the inspector raise long, skinny arms high. He cautiously poked at the security chief's lateral folds to make sure he had no hidden weapons there. Keek wriggled. This close, Han could read Keek's medals. Either these, too, had been obtained secondhand, he thought, or the inspector was also spelling champ of the planet Oor VII.

"All right, into the forward compartment there. Best behavior now; I've had all the games I'm going to play today."

Entering the forward compartment, Keek gazed without comment at Hissal, who was seated in an ac-celeration chair near the holo-gameboard. The inspec-tor found his own seat by the tech station. Bollux had seated himself on the curved acceleration couch be-hind the gameboard.

Han rested one hip on the gleaming gameboard. "Now, what's the hitch? I've got my clearances. The Imperials aren't going to be too happy about you local enforcers trying to hijack an authorized ship-ment."

Keek spoke with forced jocularity, "Ah, you

scaredy-*norg* human. Nothing's wrong! The benevolent Inner Council held an emergency session when word of this transaction reached them and placed all teaching materials and off-world literature on the restricted list." He waved the beribboned scroll. "I have here the Edict, which I am to present to you."

"And just who's the flaming Inner Council? Listen, slim, no little slowpoke world alters Imperial trade agreements." That he himself had often broken Imperial laws—shattered them to fragments would be more accurate—was something he chose not to mention.

"We are merely here, my troops and I," Keek replied evenly, "to take temporary custody of the cargo in question, until a Tion representative and an Imperial adjudicator can be summoned. The arrests were strictly an internal matter."

And the Tion representative and the Imperial adjudicator would undoubtedly come with price tags attached, Han reflected. "So who pays me?"

Keek attempted to smile; he looked preposterous. "Our supply of Imperial currency is depleted just now, due to repairs to our spacefleet. But our Treasury's note, or our planetary currency—"

"No play money!" Han exploded. "I want my cargo back. And besides, one run-down gunboat is no *spacefleet*."

"Impossible. The cargo is evidence for the trial of certain seditionists, one of whom you've been deceived into sheltering. Come, Captain; cooperate, and you'll be well received here." Keek winked, with effort. "Come! We'll pass intoxicating liquids through our bodies and boast of our sporting abilities! Let us be jolly and clumsy, as humans love to be!"

Han, who hated being played for a sucker worse than anything, gritted his teeth. "I told you already, I don't want any of your homemade cash—"

A sudden thought struck him, and he jumped up. "You want part of my cargo? Keep it! But I'm going to come across to Hissal with what's left."

The security chief seemed amused. "You seek to

extort me with educational materials? Come, Captain; we're both worldly chaps."

Han ignored Keek's attempt at flattery. Carrying a power prybar, he began breaking packing straps from a crate on the hand truck. "This is a duplicator, just the thing to set up a college press with. But it's a top-of-the-line model, and it's versatile. Hissal, I'll take that tip after all."

Confused, Hissal handed over the Brigian currency. Han showed them one of the duplicator's components.

"This is the prototyper; you can program it for what you want or feed it a sample. Like this." He inserted a Brigian bill and punched several buttons. The prototyper whirred, lights blinked, and the original bill reappeared together with an identical copy. Han held it up to the light, eyeing the duplicate critically. Keek made choking sounds, comprehending now that the pilot was holding his planet's entire monetary system hostage.

"*Hmm*. Not perfect," Han noted, "but if you supplied the machine with local materials, it would work. And for different serial numbers on each bill you just program that into the machine. That consulting firm must've been a cut-rate operation; they didn't even bother to set up a secure currency." The New Regime had obviously been the victim of aggressive salesmanship. "Well, Keek, what do you—"

Keek had snapped the end off his scroll's wooden core and pointed it directly at Han, who didn't doubt for a second that he was looking down the barrel of a gun.

"Lay your pistol on that table, alien primate," hissed Keek. "You will now have your automaton take the hand truck and he, you, and the traitor Hissal will precede me down the ramp."

Han gave Bollux the order as he carefully put his blaster on the gameboard, knowing Keek would shoot him if he tried to warn Chewbacca. But as Keek reached to take possession of the blaster, Han inconspicuously touched the gameboard's master control.

Miniature holo-monsters leaped into existence, weird creatures of a dozen worlds, spitting and striking, roaring and hopping. Keek jumped back in surprise, firing his scroll-weapon by reflex. A beam of orange energy crashed into the board, and the monsters evaporated into nothingness.

At the same instant Han, with a star-pilot's reflexes, threw himself onto the security chief, catching hold of the hand holding the scroll-gun. He groped for his blaster with his free hand, but Keek's shot had knocked it from the gameboard.

The security chief possessed incredible strength. Not stopped by the pilot's desperate punches, Keek hurled him halfway across the compartment and brought his weapon around. Just then Hissal landed on his shoulders, making Keek stagger against the edge of the acceleration couch. The two Brigians struggled, their arms and legs intertwining like a confusion of snakes.

But Keek was stronger than the smaller Hissal. Bit by bit he brought his weapon around for a shot. Han got back into the fight with a side-on kick that knocked the scroll aside so that the charge meant for Hissal burned a deep hole in one of the safety cushions.

The scroll-gun was apparently spent, and Keek began to club Hissal with it. Han tried to block him, but Keek knocked the pilot to the deck with stunning force, then turned to grapple with the other Brigian, their feet shuffling and kicking around the downed human. Unable to get around them and recover his blaster, Han tripped Keek. The inspector sank, taking Hissal with him.

Suddenly the scroll, which Keek had dropped, rolled into Han's palm. As Keek was kneeling over the fallen Hissal, Han swung the scroll, connecting solidly with the security chief's skull. Keek's lank body shook with spasms and stiffened. Hissal merely pushed him, and the security chief toppled to the deck.

A roar came from behind them. Chewbacca, seeing his partner unharmed, was visibly relieved. "Where were *you?*" Han cried. "He just about put out my running lights!" Rubbing the bruises he had received, Han recovered his pistol.

Hissal, collapsed in an acceleration chair, tried to catch his breath. "This isn't my usual line of endeavor, Captain. Thank you."

"We're sort of even," Han replied with a laugh. Keek began to stir, and Chewbacca the Wookiee snatched him to his feet with one hand. Keek, strong as he was, had better sense than to resist an enraged Wookiee.

Han covered Keek's small bud of a nose with the muzzle of his blaster. The security chief's bulging eyes crossed, watching the weapon. "That little trick of yours wasn't nice, Keek; I hate sneaks even more than hijackers. I want Hissal's people and my cargo back onboard this ship in five minutes or else you're going to have the wind whistling through your ears."

When Hissal's freed colleagues and the controversial cargo were back onboard, Han brought Keek to the ramp's head. "The Empire will hear of this," the Brigian vowed. "It's the death sentence for you."

"I'll try not to lose sleep over it," Han replied dryly. With the ship's forged papers he had used this trip, he doubted any law agency would be able to trace him. Moreover this would be, by the preoccupied Empire's lights, a very minor incident. "And do yourself a favor: don't try anything funny when you get clear. There's nothing on this planet with enough fire power to take this ship, but you might make me mad."

Keek looked at the other Brigians. "What of them?"

Han sounded casual. "Oh, I'll drop them off somewhere away from the noise and the crowds. It's legal; a spacer can contract for a surface-to-surface hop if he wants. We're going to take a long orbit, so Hissal can try out his broadcasting rig, hook it into ship's power systems."

Keek was no fool. "With that much altitude and power, he'll be reaching every receiver on the planet!"

"And what do you think he'll say?" Han asked innocently. "Something about what the New Regime's pulling? It's nothing to me, of course, but I told you pulling a gun on me would be a mistake. I'd be thinking about early retirement if I were you."

Chewbacca gave the security chief a shove to start

him on his way. Han closed the hatch. "By the way," he called over to Bollux, "thanks for handing me that scroll during the fight."

The droid replied with characteristic modesty. "After all, sir, the inspector had said it was for you. I can only hope there'll be no repercussions, Captain."

"What for?"

"For destabilizing a planetary government to get even for having your ship shot up, sir."

"Serves them right for cheating!" Han Solo declared.

☐ III

HAN stepped into the sunlight of Rudrig's brief afternoon with the balance of his pay safe in his pocket. Around him the spires, domes, towers, and other buildings that housed this part of the university stood in harmony with the lacy flowers, thick-boled trees, and purple lawns.

The university made use, in one fashion or another, of the entire planet. Its vast campuses and housing, recreation, and field training sectors were scattered over the globe. Students from all over the Tion Hegemony were compelled to come here or else leave the Tion entirely if they wanted advanced education of top quality. Centralization wasn't the best method of offering schooling, Han supposed, but was symptomatic of the languid, inept Hegemony.

He idly studied passers-by for a moment, noting many species flocking between classes, holding conversations, or playing assorted sports and various instruments. Stepping gingerly across a broad boulevard between rolling service automata, quiet mass-transit vehicles, and small ground-effect cargo transporters, he ascended a low access platform and boarded a local passenger beltway. It zipped him along between huge lecture halls and auditoriums, theaters, administrative buildings, a clinic, and a variety of classroom configurations.

Reading the glowing route markers and recalling the coordinates he had memorized from a holo-map, he stepped off the beltway again at that sector's spa, an annex of its sprawling recreation center. He had just started for the spa when he heard a voice. "Hey there, Slick!"

Han hadn't gone by that nickname in many years. Still, as he turned he kept his right hand high and near his left lapel. Though the carrying of weapons was prohibited on this quiet world, having one, Han's pragmatic philosophy ran, was a risk he was willing to take. His blaster was suspended slantwise, grip lowermost, under his left armpit and was concealed by his vest.

"Badure!" His right hand moved away from his blaster and closed in a grip on that of the old man who had called him. He used Badure's own nickname, "Trooper! What are you doing here?"

The other was a big man with a full head of hair going white, a sly squint, and a belly that had come to overlap his belt in recent years. He stood half a head taller than Han, and his grip made the younger man wince.

"Looking for you, son," Badure responded in the gravelly voice Han recalled so well. "You're showing up good, Han, real good. It must be a Wookiee's age since I've seen you. Which reminds me, how is Chewie? I was trying to find you two, and they said at the spaceport that the Wook rented a groundcoach and left word for it to be dropped off here."

Badure—Trooper—was a friend of long standing, but he seemed to have come on hard times. Han tried not to take notice of his faded, patched laborer's tunic and trousers or the scuffed and torn work boots. Still, Badure had held on to his old flight jacket, covered with its unit insignia and theater patches, and his jaunty, sweat-stained beret with its fighter-wing flash. "But how'd you know we were here?"

Badure laughed, his belly rolling. "I keep track of landings and departures, Slick. But in this case I knew you were coming."

Much as he liked this old man, Han was suspicious. "Maybe you'd better tell me more, Badure."

He looked pleased with himself. "How do you think those university types got your name, son? Not that it doesn't get around as is; I heard about that stunt at the Saheelindeeli airshow—and some rumors from out in the Corporate Sector, and something about water

smuggled down the Rampa Rapids. I was here track-
ing down a few things on my own and heard someone
was asking about capable skippers and fast ships. I
passed your name along. But before we go into that,
shouldn't you be saying hello to my business partner
here?"

Han had been so preoccupied that he had ignored
the person standing beside Badure. Chiding himself
silently for this unusual lapse in caution, he looked her
over.

The girl was short and slender, not long into
womanhood, with a pale face and disorderly red hair
that hung limply. Her brows and lashes were so light
that they scarcely showed. She wore a drab, baggy
brown outfit of pullover and pants, and her shoes appeared to be a size too large. Her hands had seen hard
work. Han had met many men and women just like
her, each bearing the stamp of the factory drone or
mining-camp worker, lowest-echelon tech or other
toiler.

She in turn studied him with no approval whatsoever. "This is Hasti," Badure said. "She already knows
your name." Indicating the flow of beings moving
around them to and from the busy spa, he gestured
that they continue toward the entrance.

Han acceded, moving slowly, but a sideways slide of
the older man's eyes confirmed something. "What do I
watch for?" he inquired simply.

Badure laughed and said, more to himself than to
Han or Hasti, "Same old Han Solo, a one-man sensor
suite."

Han's thoughts were on Badure. The man had been
his friend many years before and his partner on various enterprises a number of times since. Once, in an
uncomfortable situation stemming from an abortive
Kessel spice run, Badure had saved both Han's and
Chewbacca's lives. That he should have sought them
out here could mean only one thing.

"I won't waste your time, kid," Badure said. "There
are some that would like to see my hide hung out to
dry. I need a ship with punch, and gait to spare, and a
skipper I can trust."

Han realized that Badure wasn't going to be first to mention the life-debt the two partners owed him. "You want us to put our necks in the slot for you, is that it? Trooper, saving someone's life doesn't give you the right to risk it again. We're finally ahead of the game; do we owe it all out again this soon?"

Badure countered in neutral tones. "You're answering for the Wook, too, Han?"

"Chewie'll see it my way." *If I have to reason with him with a wrench!*

Hašti joined the conversation for the first time. *"Now* are you satisfied, Badure?" she asked bitterly.

The old man hushed her gently. To Han he went on, "I'm not asking you two to work for nothing. There'd be a cut—"

"The thing is, we're flush. Uh, in fact, we can cut some loose to see you through for a while."

He felt he had gone too far and thought for a moment that Badure was going to swing at him. The old man had made and spent a number of fortunes and had always been open-handed to his friends; but the offer of charity to himself had the ring of an insult. Favoring Han with a venomous look, Hasti put a hand on Badure's arm. "We're wasting time; our luggage is still at the district hostelry."

"Clear skies, Han," Badure said in a quiet voice, "and to the Wook as well."

Han gazed after the two long after they had disappeared on a passenger beltway.

Determined to put the incident out of his mind, he entered the spa. It offered specific creature comforts to a huge variety of human, humanoid, and nonhumanoid species. There were zero-gee massagers, ozone chambers, effluvial rinses, and many other options for humans; mud tanks for visiting Draflago; dermal autostrippers to service a Lisst'n or Pui-Ui; gill-flushes for any of a number of piscine or amphibian life forms; and as many other ablutive and restorative amenities as could be packed into the huge complex.

Inquiring at the central information area, Han discovered that Chewbacca was still enjoying the pleasures of a full-service grooming. Han himself had meant to take a leisurely cycle of soaking, sauna, massage, and pore cleansing, followed by a visit to the tonsorial center. But his encounter with Badure and Hasti left him feeling in need of a more active and distracting program.

He undressed in a private booth, storing gun and other valuables in a lockbox and feeding his pleated dress shirt, clothes, and boots to an autovalet. Then he dropped several coins into the slot of an omniron and stepped inside, keying it for maximum treatment.

In fifteen-second cycles icy water sprayed at him, sonics vibrated his skin and flesh, waves of heat lashed and nearly seared him, needle-streams of bio-detergents lathered him, walls of swirling foam broke and surged through the cubicle, air nozzles hosed their blasts, and emollients were rubbed on him by vigorous autoapplicators.

He withstood the brunt of these processes and took on more cycles, finding he couldn't shake the image of Badure. Telling himself he had done the shrewd thing did no more to improve his state of mind than did the elaborate bubble bath he was taking, he concluded. So he terminated the omniron's program short of its allotted time, recovered his cleaned clothing and shined boots from the autovalet, donned his blaster, and resettled his vest. Then he set off to find his partner.

Chewbacca was in the portion of the spa reserved for its more hirsute clientele. Following the light-strip directory system helpfully placed along the floors, Han found his friend's treatment room. Checking the room's monitoring screen, he saw the Wookiee floating in a zero-gee field, arms and legs splayed. He was near the end of his session; every individual hair had been given a light mutual-repulsion charge to separate it while dirt, particulate matter, and old oils were removed. Now new oils and conditioners were being gently applied. Chewbacca wore a toothy grin, luxu-riating in the treatment as he floated like a tremendous stuffed toy, his billowing pelt making him seem twice his normal girth.

Turning from the screen, Han noticed two very ap-

pealing young human females who were also waiting.
One, a tall blonde in an expensive jumpsuit, spoke
into the ear of her companion, a shorter girl with ring-
lets of brown hair. The second girl wore a sportier outfit of shorts and singlet; she eyed Han speculatively.
"Are you here to meet Captain Chewbacca, sir?"

Mystified, Han repeated, *"Captain . . ."*

"Chewbacca. We saw him walking across campus
and we had to stop him and talk. We're both taking
courses in nonhuman sociology, and we couldn't pass
up the chance. We've studied the Wookiee language
tapes a little, so we understood a bit. Captain Chewbacca told us his copilot would be coming by to meet
him. He invited us to go with you on a groundcoach
ride."

Han smiled in spite of himself. "Fine with me. I'm
Captain Chewbacca's first mate, Han Solo."

He had just established that the brunette's name
was Viurre and her blond girlfriend's Kiili when
Chewbacca emerged from the treatment room. The
Wookiee, settling his admiral's hat on his head at a
rakish angle, wore a beatific grin; his shaggy coat, now
glistening and lustrous, floated lightly on stray air currents.

Han sketched a sarcastic salute. *"Captain* Chewbacca, sir, I've got the whole crew standing by for
orders."

The Wookiee *wuff*ed in confusion, then, remembering his assumed role, rumbled a vague reply that none
of them understood. The girls promptly forgot Han
and closed in on the Wookiee, complimenting him on
his appearance. "I believe you ordered a groundcoach,
Skipper?" hinted Han.

His partner *awoo*ed confirmation, and they all set
off. "What have you found to be the essential dif-
ferences in the life-experience on Wookiee worlds?"
Viurre asked Han earnestly.

"The tables are higher off the floor," the pilot replied without expression.

When they arrived at the carport, Han goggled
and shouted, "Tell me this is the wrong slip!" Kiili and

Viurre "oohed" in delight, while Chewbacca beamed fondly at the vehicle he had selected.

It was over eight meters long, wide and low to the ground. The groundcoach's sides, rear deck, and hood were paneled in dazzling scarlet *greel* wood that had been lacquered and polished and lacquered over and over until its metallic gleam seemed to go on forever through the fine grain. The coach's trim, bumpers, door hinges, latches, and handles were of silver alloy. It boasted an outlandish crystal hood ornament— frolicking nymphs in a swirl of gauzy, windblown veil- dresses.

The driver's seat was open to the weather, but just behind it and a luggage well was an enclosed pas- senger cab, also paneled in *greel* wood, complete with elaborate, hanging road lamps, tasseled bunting, and running boards and handrails on either side for foot- men. Astern the cab was another luggage well between a pair of ludicrous meter-high tail fins bejeweled with all manner of signaling and warning lights. From the coach's primary and secondary antenna whips fluttered two pennants, several streamers, and the furry tail of some small, luckless animal.

"Too austere," Han muttered sarcastically, but he couldn't resist popping the coach's hood. A massive, fiendishly complicated engine squatted there. But Chewbacca quickly silenced Han's denunciations and amazed the two girls by throwing open the cover of the midship luggage well. It contained, due to his thoughtful arrangement, a heroic picnic lunch.

Kiili and Viurre had piled into the driver's com- partment, investigating controls, dials, the sound sys- tem, and stowage drawers. Chewbacca was running an adoring palm over a quarter-panel when Han blurted out, "I bumped into Badure today, just as I was coming into the spa."

Forgetting everything else, Chewbacca barked a question. Han glanced away. "He wanted to hire us, but I told him we didn't need the work." Then he felt compelled to add, "Well, we don't, do we?"

Chewbacca howled furiously. The two girls studi- ously ignored the argument. *"What* do we owe

Badure?" Han hollered back. "He made a business offer, Chewie." But he knew better. *Wookiees will honor a Life-Debt over anything else; he'll never walk away from it,* Han thought. Chewbacca growled another angry comment.

"What if I don't want to? Are you going to go after him without me?" Han asked, knowing what the answer would be.

The Wookiee regarded him for a long moment, then uttered a deep *Uurrr?*

Han opened his mouth, closed it, then finally answered. "No, you won't have to. Get in the bus."

Chewbacca yipped, knuckled Han's shoulder, ambled off around the coach's stern, and climbed in. Han slid into the driver's seat and swung his door shut.

"Captain Chewbacca and I have to go track down a pal," he told Kiili and Viurre brusquely. Then to himself he added, *I knew this would happen; I never should have told Chewie. So why did I?*

Kiili, twirling blond hair around one finger, smiled. "First Mate Solo, what should we talk to the captain about?"

"Anything. He just likes to listen to people talk." Han gunned the engine and expertly pulled the powerful coach out of its parking slip. "Tell him how he's ruining a great afternoon," Han encouraged her, then smiled. "Or sing some off-color ditties, if you know any."

Kiili eyed the contented Wookiee uncertainly. *"He* likes *those?"*

Han smiled engagingly. "No. I do."

☐ IV

REMEMBERING that Hasti, the young woman with Badure, had mentioned the district hostelry, Han zoomed off in that direction. The scarlet monstrosity of a coach, riding its low ground-effect cushion, handled smoothly and responded well for its size.

One long arm along the back of the driver's seat, Chewbacca tilted his admiral's cap down and listened while Kiili and Viurre described the life of an undergraduate student of nonhuman sociology.

They didn't have to enter the hostelry. Badure and Hasti were waiting at an intercampus shuttleskimmer stop near the building. Han pulled over to the curb with a belch of braking thrust, and he and Chewbacca jumped out, followed by the two girls. The Wookiee hugged the old man giving out joyous sounds. Hasti regarded Han coolly. "Attack of conscience?"

Han angled a thumb at the Wookiee. "My partner's a sentimental fellow. Do you feel like telling us what we're getting into?"

Indicating Viurre and Kiili with a slight nod, Badure cleared his throat meaningfully. Viurre took the hint and, dragging the tall blond with her, was suddenly inspired to inspect some nearby foliage. In confidential tones Badure asked Han, "You must've heard of the ship called the *Queen of Ranroon?*"

Chewbacca quivered his nose in surprise, and Han's eyebrows shot up. "The treasure ship? The story they use to put kids to bed?"

"Not story," Badure corrected, *"history.* The *Queen of Ranroon* was crammed full with spoils from whole solar systems, tribute to Xim the Despot."

"Listen, Badure, crazies have been hunting that

ship for centuries. If she ever existed, she was either destroyed or someone plundered her long ago. You've been watching too many holo-thrillers."

"When did I ever go chasing vacuum?" the old man countered.

A good point. "You know where the *Queen* is? You've got proof?"

"I know where her log-recorder is," Badure announced so confidently that Han found himself believing it. The vision of a treasure arose, a treasure so stupendous that it had become a synonym for phenomenal wealth, more than a man might squander in many lifetimes. . . .

"Let's get going," Han proposed. "We're not getting any younger." Hasti's derisive look didn't faze him. Then he noticed that Badure's face was drawn with tension.

Following his gaze, Han turned to see a black groundlimo slowly cruising toward them. Han drew Badure over to the coach, encouraging Hasti to move as well with an inclination of the head. Chewbacca, who had already thrown Badure's and Hasti's light baggage into the passenger cab, was also on the alert.

Someone in the limo had noticed their reaction. The black groundcar accelerated sharply and veered straight at them.

"Everybody into the coach," Han yelled as the limo jumped the curb and screeched to a stop, blocking the coach's front cowling. Badure began pushing Hasti into the coach's front seat as Chewbacca, unable to carry his bowcaster on this peaceful world, glanced around for a makeshift weapon.

Figures tumbled from the limo as Han drew his blaster. The blue concentric rings of a stun charge reached out and caught Badure, who had just propelled Hasti out of the way. She fell backward across the seat; Badure staggered. She managed to grab him and pull him onto the driver's seat just as Han fired an answering shot.

By then a half-dozen beings had emerged from the limo with weapons of one kind or another. Han's hasty return shot caught the stun-gunner, a red-beaked humanoid, in its long, feathered arm. Two male humans armed with needlebeamers•ducked as Han's shots shattered two of the limo's windows. The assailants, seeing that they had a fight on their hands, made a general migration toward the ground.

Chewbacca was clambering over the midship luggage well to help Hasti when she, hanging on to Badure with one hand, kicked the engine over and threw the scarlet coach into reverse. Two of the attackers who had been closing in found themselves pouncing on empty air. With a tremendous bump, the coach climbed the curb in reverse. Chewbacca had to cling to a decorative lantern to save himself, and Han jumped aside to keep from being run down, as Hasti hit braking thrusters, kicking up clots of purplish turf and exposing the rich gray soil of Rudrig.

"Well, pile on, Solo," she shouted at Han. He barely got to a running board, seizing a footman's handrail, before the coach surged forward.

Hasti didn't quite clear the end of the obstructing limo. The coach bashed it aside, half-rotating the black vehicle and crunching in its own nose cowling with a shower of *greel* wood fragments. Chewbacca cried out at the damage. As they lurched past, Han directed a suppressive barrage at the limo and its passengers, more intent on clinging to his life than on accuracy.

Hasti swerved to avoid a robo-delivery truck, thereby slamming Han up against the cab and nearly wrenching Chewbacca from the lamp, flipping him over with a snap that twisted his neck and sent his prized admiral's hat flying in the breeze. The Wookiee keened, grief-stricken, for the lost headgear.

Over the howl of the coach's engine and the blast of its slipstream, Han yelled, "They're coming after us!"

The black limo was already slewing around to give chase. Han brought his blaster up. At that moment Hasti, ignoring a traffic-robo, tore into an intersection directly toward a slow-moving maintenance hauler that was towing a disabled freight droid. The girl set all her weight against the steering-grip yoke and hit the coach's warning horn. The first two bars of the

Rudrig University Anthem sounded majestically from the coach's fractured hood. The maintenance hauler dodged with a bleep of distress and barely missed taking the driver's side off the coach.

The coach streaked straight down the thoroughfare now. Holding his abused neck stiffly, Chewbacca began inching forward again in order to take over the driving duties. A double column of students and visitors on an orientation tour chose that moment to enter a crosswalk, and Hasti hit braking thrusters.

Chewbacca flew head-first into the driver's compartment and hit the floor, his feet sticking up into the air. But even under those conditions, he had the presence of mind to notice that Badure wasn't completely aboard, and he clutched the stunned man's clothing to tug him into the coach. Hasti noticed her companion's dilemma and gave the coach a snappy cut so that the passenger door swung shut. Though hampered by wires of pain lancing through his neck, the Wookiee began extricating himself.

Just astern, Han had managed to pull himself inside the passenger cab and saw that the limo was closing in rapidly. He smashed the cab's crystalline rear window with a hard blow from his blaster. It cracked in webs, split, and fell away. Clearing away the shards, Han leaned his forearms across the empty sill. The coach's bouncing made the macro-sights useless, so he waited for a clear shot.

Chewbacca had hauled himself up and was yelping loudly at Hasti and gesturing madly. She somehow understood his meaning and hit the couch adjustment controls, which started up the servo-motors. Hasti held tightly to the control stem as the couch moved from under her, leaving her in a tense stoop. The Wookiee slid in behind her, whisked her out of the way, then took over the controls. Hasti turned at once and saw to her relief that Badure was unhurt. He was already stirring, throwing off the stun charge's effects.

The Wookiee proceeded directly through an intersection without benefit of right of way, aware that the limo, still chasing the coach, was zooming along between towering buildings.

Taking a fast curve, Chewbacca came abruptly up to a road-repair site. Far back in the mirror's reflection he could see the limo closing in. He gunned the engine, bursting through illumi-panel markers, smashing warning light-banks aside, and hurling two robo-flagwavers, still diligently waving their flags, several meters into the air. But his hopes for a safe route through the site were dashed when he rounded the turn; the roadbed had been excavated completely, side to side, the shoulders torn up right up to the building faces.

Chewbacca slowed, calmly considered his options, and decided he would have to offer his pursuers a head-on challenge. He hit the accelerator and swung the steering grips over for a smuggler's turn. The long coach leaped forward into a precise end-for-end spin, destroying several more danger indicators, its lift cushion kicking up dirt and debris. Then it sped off in the direction from which it had come.

Han leaned out a side window. As the limo bore down on them he propped his forearm through a handrail and opened fire, scoring hits on the limo's hood and one in the center of its windshield. Prepared for a terrible impact, Chewbacca uttered a piercing cry and Hasti began hugging Badure. Han could make out terrified expressions among the limo's occupants.

At the last moment the limo driver wavered, declining the imminent head-on, and the black vehicle swung aside. Ripping through a dense Mullanite lattice-sculpture of thick creepers, slewing across a stretch of purple lawn, and—after bowling aside several long planters and snapping support columns—the limo ended up on a portico outside the local Curriculum Committee headquarters.

Chewbacca brayed his delight, but Han called a warning as the limo started up again. Chewbacca, glancing at the several rearview mirrors and single aft viewscreen, made a hard right turn to high speed by dint of sheer strength applied to unwilling controls.

The coach's left side rose, and the Wookiee took advantage of his momentum to snag another quick right into a side avenue, hoping to break off the chase.

Unfortunately, he had swung the long coach onto the up-ramp of a major ground-transport artery. But he had the presence of mind to apply a Han Solo adage: when it won't help to slow down, pour it on! So he slapped toggle switches for full boost and auxiliary guidance thrust.

The immediate problem was a refuse-collection robo-dumpster making its way up the ramp. Its cyber-pilot system was in a quandary over this unusual obstruction. Chewbacca, still exploiting centrifugal force, hit his offside thrusters and took the groundcoach full tilt against the ramp's safety fence.

The fence, part of a traffic-control design scheme based on very forgiving systems, gave and bent outward as the Wookiee barreled along with half the coach on the ground, half up on the wilting fence. Han, dragging himself up off the cab floorboards, took one look ahead and hit the deck again. The robo-dumpster edged toward the opposite side of the up-ramp and the two weighty vehicles passed each other.

The coach had lost its outermost rearview mirror post and part of the picnic lunch, and debris from the jostled dumpster was splattered across its meter-high red tail fins. Chewbacca was baying in utter exhilaration, an ages-old Wookiee war cry.

Hasti had just finished fastening a seatbelt across herself and Badure when the coach roared onto the main artery. Seeing that he was heading the wrong way on a high-speed road, the Wookiee hugged the outside wall while he assessed his situation. He kept one finger on the horn button, sounding the first two bars of the anthem over and over. All factors considered, Chewbacca felt, things were going fairly well.

Han, back in the passenger cab, held a somewhat different opinion. The black limo had taken advantage of Chewbacca's descent and was still on their tail. The intercom wasn't working, so Han pushed up the cab's forward window and shouted, "They're still on us!"

The Wookiee growled an irritated reply, then spotted his opening. He turned the steering grips with such emphasis that the yoke groaned on its stem, threatening to snap. But the coach managed to fishtail across three lanes of oncoming traffic, and Chewbacca hung in the center lane while awaiting shifts in the configuration of the traffic.

Automatic safety systems had taken notice of the potential massacre, and suddenly sequential warning lights began to flash, cautioning other drivers where the danger lay. Overhead illumi-markers and danger panels began flashing along the way, and those vehicles operating under autocontrol were brought to a halt at the shoulder by Traffic Central Override.

Meanwhile, Han, clinging to the rear window frame, saw the limo coming on. Its driver was having an easier time, following the trail the Wookiee had blazed. Han braced his right shoulder against one side of the frame and his left hand against the other to draw a steady aim. Just as he fired, Chewbacca, having lined up another gap in the oncoming traffic, hauled at the steering grips and cut hard for the center divider. Han's shot went wild, blowing a small hole in the tough fusionformed road.

Chewbacca came at the divider as directly as he could, aware that it was built to resist collision. He hit it with the coach's accelerator open, keeping his enormous foot down hard on emergency-boost auxiliaries. The engine wailed. Hasti clung to Badure.

The coach burst through a double retaining rail, taking two lengths of railing with it. Chewbacca then swooped up the sloped center abutment; two lanterns fell from the coach, and its curb feelers, he noticed, had been sheared off. Han tangled both fists into embroidered safety belting and set his feet against the cab's front wall.

The coach shot through the fence at the top of the abutment, the durable links stretching, then bursting with a titanic jolt that sent the remainder of the picnic lunch arcing into the air. Crashing down the abutment and through a second section of railing, they bounced into the traffic lanes now headed in the appropriate direction, if at illegal velocity.

Maneuvering smartly, the Wookiee avoided any other collisions. The coach sped along, intermittently shedding trim and pieces of smashed *greel* wood.

Glancing out a side window, Han found himself the object of the surprised scrutiny of a gowned senior professor, a stalk-eyed creature in a robo-hack. Chewbacca accelerated and left the hack behind.

Less than a minute later, the black limo appeared at the crest of the abutment and descended through the swath of destruction left by Chewbacca. It, too, slid into the traffic lanes. A man, holding a long needlebeam rifle in his hands, stood up and poked his head and arms through the sunroof.

Han left the cab, swung from the handrail with one foot on the running board, and dove into the driver's compartment. "We've gone and made them mad," he hollered. "Escape and evade, old buddy!"

But even as Han exhorted his partner, Chewbacca was throwing the coach through zigs and zags, ignoring lane divider illumi-strips, applying full power though a disconcerting black smoke had begun to roil from the vehicle's engine. At last, the rifleman, his eye at his weapon's scope, fired.

A needlebeam sizzled at one of the scarlet tail fins, setting the lacquered wood afire and shearing off its tip as taillight circuitry blew. Han stood up, one hand firmly on the windshield and blaster gripped in the other. He replied with a hurried shot of his own; the bolt splashed harmlessly onto the pavement.

A second rifle beam hissed through the cab. "Get us out of here before they cut us in half!" Han yelled to his first mate.

Smoke from the hood now rolled more thickly. The Wookiee spun the steering-grip yoke, veering and putting an enormous robo-freighthauler between the coach and the limo. Another needlebeam, missing them, burned across the freighthauler's rear end. The last view Han had of the limo was of its driver trying to maneuver for another clear shot. He shouted to Chewbacca, "Pump your braking thrusters!" The Wookiee did so without question, accustomed to his friend's mad inspirations. When the freighthauler outstripped the coach, they found themselves even with the limo.

The surprised rifleman started to bring his weapon

up, but Han fired first. The marksman, clutching his smoldering forearm, dropped back through the sunroof. Han's second shot blew out a piece of the limo's door. Two or three beings were trying to elbow their way up through the sunroof to set up a rocket launcher. If they couldn't stop the coach, they'd settle for blowing it all over the landscape.

Han felt the coach surge and looked around. Directly in front of them was the freighthauler, its long rear gate bouncing on the road. Its bed was half empty, a pile of construction rubble heaped against the front wall. An overpass loomed in the distance; Han quickly grasped his first mate's plan, holstered his weapon, and clung to Badure and Hasti for his life.

The coach jumped up the hanging rear gate, engine pouring black smoke, auxiliary thrusters overloading. Chewbacca pumped braking thrusters once to time his maneuver, then hit full power and the front-lift thrusters designed to help the coach negotiate low obstacles. The coach shot up the pile of rubble at the front of the cargo bed and soared into the air, the Wookiee plying his controls frantically.

Then the overpass was beneath them, and through some miracle it was unoccupied just then. The coach hit with an impact that collapsed its shock-absorption system, burned out its power routing, broke all the remaining lanterns, and shattered the cab windows. It slid, then ground to a halt against the overpass sidewall, crumpling its hood and popping its doors.

Coughing, Han and his first mate pulled Hasti and Badure from the wreckage. The black limo was already far down the road, forced along by the flow of traffic. Chewbacca, surveying the demolished groundcoach sorrowfully, sniffled and moaned to himself.

Wiping her eyes and choking, Hasti wanted to know: "Who ever told you two morons you could drive?" Then, noticing Chewbacca's gloomy look, asked, "What's wrong with him?"

"He figures he'll have a hard time getting his deposit back," Han explained.

Police groundcruisers and aircraft, converging under Traffic Control's direction, were already beginning to gather farther down the highway. Since Chewbacca had elected to leave the road in a unique manner, it would probably take the local authorities some time to piece together what had happened.

☐ V

"QUIET down and sit still." Han took a firmer grip on his first mate's head.

The Wookiee, seated in a rump-sprung, sweat-stained acceleration chair in the *Millennium Falcon*'s forward compartment, stopped squirming but couldn't stifle his whimpers. He knew his neck injury had to be tended right away. Han, standing behind him, shuffling for a better stance, held his friend's chin clamped in one elbow. He pushed the palm of his hand against the Wookiee's skull.

"How many times have I done this now? Stop complaining!" Han began to apply pressure again, twisting Chewbacca's head up and to the left. The Wookiee dutifully fought the urge to rise, crimping his long fingers on the arms of the acceleration chair.

Meeting resistance, Han drew a deep breath and, without warning, yanked the thick-maned skull with all his might. There was a cracking and popping; Chewbacca yipped and snuffled pitifully. But when Han ruffled his friend's fur compassionately and stepped back, the Wookiee rubbed his neck and moved his head without pain. He immediately went off to prepare the starship for liftoff.

"If you're through ministering to the afflicted, Doctor," Hasti said from her seat by the gameboard, "it's time we got a few things settled."

Leaning against the tech station, Han agreed. "Let's put them on the table and see what we've got."

Badure, fully recovered from the stun charge, was sitting next to Hasti. To avoid conflict, he took over. "I met Hasti and her sister, Lanni, at a mining camp on a planet named Dellalt, here in the Tion Hegemony.

It was a small plunder operation; I was contract labor there."

He ignored Han's surprise. *Things have been worse than I thought for him,* the pilot realized.

"And things weren't too much better for them," Badure went on. "You know how those camps can be, and this one was about the worst I've seen. We three sort of watched out for one another.

"Lanni had a Pilot's Guild book and flew a lot of work runs, surface-to-surface stuff. Somewhere she had picked up a log-recorder, one of the ancient disk types. No ship has used one in centuries. She couldn't read the characters, of course, but there was a figure most beings in this part of space know, the *Queen of Ranroon.*"

"How'd a log-recorder get to Dellalt?"

"That's where the vaults are," Badure said, and that brought some history back to Han. Xim the Despot had left behind legends of whole planets despoiled, of mass spacings of prisoners and other atrocities. And Xim the Despot had ordered that stupendous treasure vaults be built for the tribute to be sent him by his conquering armies. The treasure never arrived, and the vacant vaults, all that remained from Xim's reign, were a minor curiosity generally ignored by the big, busy galaxy.

"Are you telling me the *Queen* made it to Dellalt after all?"

Badure shook his head. "But somebody made it there with the log-recorder disk."

"The disk is in a lockbox in the public storage facility that set up operations in the old vaults," Hasti told him. "My sister was afraid it would be taken from her, for the mining company runs surprise inspections, barracks searches, and sensor frisks. So she diverted course on a freight run and made the deposit."

"How'd she get it in the first place? And where is she now?" Han saw the sobering answer on both their faces and wasn't surprised. The opposition, he had already learned, was in deadly earnest. He abandoned the subject.

"So, off to Dellalt before that rental agent comes looking for his groundcoach."

But Badure, slapping his ample belly, announced, "We have one more crewman coming. He's on his way now. I canceled our public-carrier reservations so the line will refer him directly here."

"Who? What do we need him for?" Han was reluctant to involve too many in this treasure hunt.

"His name is Skynx; he's a ranking expert on pre-Republic times in this part of space. And he reads ancient languages; he's already deciphered some characters Lanni had copied from the log-recorder disk. Good enough for you?"

Conditionally. Somebody, Han saw, would have to decipher the disk to find out what had happened to the *Queen*. Removing his vest, Han began disencumbering himself of the shoulder holster. "Next question: who's the opposition?"

"The mine operators. You know how the Tion works. Somebody pays someone in the Ministry of Industry and gets a permit. The mining outfit carves up the terrain any which way, grabs what it can, and gets out long before any inspectors or legal paperwork catch up with them. They usually get their financing from some crime boss.

"This outfit's run by twins. The woman's name is J'uoch and her brother's R'all. They have a partner, Egome Fass, their enforcer. He's a big, mean humanoid, a *Houk,* even taller than Chewie there. All three came up the hard way, and that's how they play."

Han had buckled on his gunbelt and holster and transferred his blaster. "So I saw. And all you want is for us to get you to Dellalt and get you off?"

Just then the intercom carried the Wookiee's news that someone was signaling for permission to board. "That'll be Skynx," Badure told him. Han passed word to admit the academician.

"If you'll get us to the vaults and off Dellalt again," Badure resumed, "I'll pay you twice your usual first-asking price, out of the treasure. But if you throw in with us, you and the Wook can split a full share of the take."

Hasti cried, "Half-share!" just as Han protested, "Full share each!" They glared at each other. "Wound up a little too tight are we, sweetheart?" Han asked. "How're you going to get there without us, flap your arms?" He heard Chewbacca's footsteps moving toward the main hatch.

Hasti's temper flared. "For one hop, you and that furball want a full cut?"

Badure held up his hands and bellowed, *"Enough!"* They quieted. "That's nicer, kiddies. We are discussing major cash here, plenty for everybody. The breakdown's this way: a full share for me because I got Hasti off Dellalt alive and Lanni passed what she knew along to both of us, equally. Two shares for Hasti, her own and poor Lanni's. And for you, Skynx, and the Wook, half-shares each at this point. Depending on who has to do what in the course of finding that treasure, we renegotiate. Agreed?"

Han studied Badure and the seething red-haired girl. "How much are we talking about?" he wanted to know.

The old man inclined his head. "Why not ask him?"

Badure indicated the individual who had come onboard and was following Chewbacca into the forward compartment. *Now why did I assume he'd be human?* Han wondered.

Skynx was a Ruurian, of average size—a little over a meter long—low to the ground, his natural coat a thick, woolly amber with bands of brown and red. He moved on eight pairs of short limbs with a graceful, rippling motion. Feathery, bobbing antennae curled back from his head. Skynx had big, multifaceted red eyes, a tiny mouth, and small nostrils. Behind him rolled a baggage-robo with several crates and boxes on its flatbed.

Skynx paused and reared up on his last four pairs of extremities. The digits on his limbs, four apiece, were mutually opposable, deft, and very versatile. He waved to the humans. "Ah, Badure," he called in a rapid, high-pitched voice, "and the lovely Hasti; how are you, young lady? This fine Wookiee I've already met. So you would be our captain, sir?"

"Would be? I *am*. Han Solo."

"Delighted! I am Skynx of Ruuria, Human History subdepartment, pre-Republic subdivision, whose chair I currently hold."

"What do you use it for?" Han asked, eying Skynx's strange anatomy. Seeing no reason to delay where cash was concerned, he inquired, "How much money are we after?"

Skynx poised his head in thought. "There's so much conflicting information about the *Queen of Ranroon,* it's best to say this: Xim the Despot's treasure vessel was the largest ship ever built in her day. Your guess, sir, is no less plausible than my own."

Han leaned back and thought about pleasure palaces, gambling planets, star yachts, and all the women of the galaxy who hadn't been fortunate enough to make his acquaintance. Yet. Chewbacca snorted and returned to the cockpit.

"Count us in," Han announced. "Tell the baggage clunker to leave your stuff right there, Skynx. Badure, Hasti, make yourselves at home."

Hasti and Skynx both wanted to watch the liftoff from the cockpit. When they were alone, Badure spoke more confidentially. "There's one thing I didn't want the others to hear, Han. I had my ear to the ground, heard about some of the crazy jobs you've pulled. Word's out that somebody's looking for you. Money's being spread around, but I haven't heard any names. Any idea who it might be?"

"Half the galaxy, it feels like sometimes." There had been many runs, many deals, jobs, and foul-ups. "How should *I* know?" But his expression hardened, and Badure thought Han had a very good idea who might be seeking him.

Han stood in the middle of the forward compartment, listening. The tech station and most of the other equipment in the compartment had been shut down to lower the noise level. He could feel the vibrations of the *Millennium Falcon*'s engines. He heard a quiet sound behind him.

Han spun, crouching, in execution of the speedraw, firing from the hip. The target-remote, a small globe that moved on squirts of repulsor power and puffs of forced air, didn't quite dodge his beam. Its counter-fire passed over him. Deactivated by his harmless tracer beam, the orb hung immobile, awaiting another practice sequence.

Han looked over to where Bollux, the labor droid, sat; his chest panels were open. Blue Max, the com-puter module installed in the droid's chest cavity, had been controlling the remote. "I told you I wanted a tougher workout than that thing's idiot circuitry could give me," Han reprimanded Blue Max.

Bollux, a gleaming, green, barrel-chested automa-ton, had arms long enough to suggest a simian. The computer, an outrageously expensive package built for maximum capacity, was painted a deep blue, whence came his name. Part of Han's post–Corporate Sector splurge had included the modification the two mechanicals had requested, because without them he and the Wookiee might never have survived. Bollux now contained a newer and more powerful receiver, and Max had been provided with a compact holo-projector.

"That *was*," the little module objected. "Can I help it if you're so flaming fast? I could cut response time to nil, if you want."

Han sighed. "No. And watch your language, Max; just because I talk like that doesn't mean you can." He took the combat charge his weapon usually carried from its case at his belt.

Badure was reclining in one of the acceleration chairs. "You've been practicing all through this run. You're beating the ballie every time. Who's got you worried?"

Han shrugged, then added as if by afterthought, "Did you ever hear of a gunman called Gallandro?"

Both of Badure's thick eyebrows rose. *"Thê* Gallandro? You don't bother yourself with small-timers, do you, Slick? So that's it."

Han looked around. Hasti, at her own and Badure's insistence, had commandeered Han's personal quarters—a cramped cubicle—for some secret purpose. Chewbacca was at the controls, but Skynx was present. Han decided it didn't matter if the Ruurian heard.

"I backed Gallandro down a while back, didn't even realize who he was. See, he had to let me do it at the time because it was part of a bigger deal he was working. Later on, though, he wanted to settle up."

Sweat gathered on his forehead with the memory. "He really *moves;* I couldn't even follow his practice draw. Anyway, I pulled a stunt on him and got out of the mess. I guess I made him look pretty bad, but I never thought he'd go to all this trouble."

"Gallandro? Slick, you're talking about the guy who single-handedly hijacked the *Quamar Messenger* on her maiden run and took over that pirate's nest, Geedon V, all by himself. And he went to the gun against the Malorm family, drawing head bounty on all five of them. And no one has ever beaten the score he rolled up when he was flying a fighter with Marso's Demons. Besides which, he's the only man who ever forced the Assassins' Guild to default on a contract; he personally canceled half of their Elite Circle—one at a time—plus assorted journeymen and apprentices."

"I know, I know," Han said wearily, sitting down, *"now.* If I'd known who he was then, I'd have put a few parsecs between us, at least. But what does a character like that want with me?"

Badure spoke as to a slow-witted child. "Han, don't make someone like Gallandro back down, then walk away making a fool of him. His kind live on their reputations. You know that as well as I do. They accept no insult and never, never back down. He'll make you his career until he settles with you."

Han sighed. "It's a big galaxy; he can't spend the rest of his life looking for me." He wished he could believe that.

There was a sound behind him, and he threw himself sideways out of his chair, firing in midair, rolling to avoid the remote's sting-shot. His tracer beam hit the dodging globe dead center. "Good try, Max," he commented.

"You strike me as being very adept, Captain," Skynx said from the padded nook over the acceleration couch.

Han climbed to his feet. "You know all about master blastermen, don't you?" He appraised the academician. "Why'd you come on this run anyway? We could've brought the disk to you."

The little Ruurian seemed embarrassed. "Er, that is, as you probably know, my species' life cycle is—"

"Never saw a Ruurian until I met you," Han interjected. "Skynx, there're more life forms in this galaxy than anyone's bothered to count, you know that. Just listing the sentient ones is a life's work."

"Of course. To explain: we Ruurians go through three separate forms after leaving the egg. There is the larva, that which you see before you; the cycle of the chrysalis, in which we undergo changes while in pupa form; and the endlife stage, in which we become chroma-wing fliers and ensure the survival of our species. The pupae are rather helpless, you'll understand, and the chroma-wings are, um, preoccupied, caring only for flight, mating, and egg-laying."

"There better be no cocoons or eggs on this ship," Han warned darkly.

"He promises," Badure said impatiently. "Now will you listen?"

Skynx resumed. "All that leaves for us larval-stage Ruurians is to protect the pupae and ensure that the simple-minded chroma-wings don't get into trouble— and to run our planet. We are very busy, right from birth."

"What's that got to do with a nice larva like you raising ship for lost treasure?" Han asked.

"I studied the histories of your own scattered species, and I came to be fascinated with this concept, *adventure,*" Skynx confessed as if unburdening himself of some dark perversity. "Of all the races who gamble their well-being on uncertain returns—and there aren't that many, statistically—the trait's most noticeable in humans, one of the most successful life forms."

Skynx tried to frame his next words carefully. "The stories, the legends, the songs, and holo-thrillers held such appeal. Once, before I spin my chrysalis, to sleep deeply and emerge a chroma-wing who will no longer be Skynx, I wish to cast aside good sense and try a human-style adventure." Saying the last, he sounded happy.

There was a silence. "Play him the song you played for me, Skynx," Badure finally invited. In the upholstered nook he had occupied for most of the trip, Skynx had set up his species' version of a storage apparatus, a treelike framework used in lieu of boxes or bags. From its various branches hung Skynx's personal possessions and items he wished to have close to him. Each artifact was an enigma, but among them was apparently at least one musical instrument.

Han had heard enough nonhuman music to want to forgo listening. Though he might be passing up decent entertainment, he might also be avoiding sounds resembling somebody's unoiled groundcoach. He changed the subject hurriedly.

"Why don't you show us what's in the crates instead?" Han looked around. "Where's Hasti? She should be in on this."

"We'll be making planetfall soon, and she has preparations to make," Badure said. "Skynx, show him those remains; they should interest him."

Skynx rose, shook out his amber coat to fluff it, and flowed smoothly out of his nook. Hoping that "remains" didn't refer to the sort of unappetizing objects he had seen in museums, Han stepped up to the crates with a power prybar. At Skynx's direction, he opened a container and whistled softly in astonishment. "Badure, give me a hand getting this thing out of the crate, will you?" Between them they strained and lifted out the object, setting it on the gameboard.

It was an automaton's head. More correctly, it was the cranial turret of some robot out of ancient history. Its optical lenses were darkened by long radiation exposure. It was armored like a dreadnought with a coarse, heavy gray alloy Han didn't recognize. The assorted insignia and tech markings engraved into its surface were still visible but readable. Han expected the speaker grille to spew a challenge.

"It's a war-robot. Xim the Despot built a brigade of them to serve as his absolutely faithful royal guard," Skynx explained. "They were, at that time, the most formidable human-form fighting machines in the galaxy. This one's remains were recovered from the floating ruins of Xim's orbital fortress, possibly the only one that wasn't vaporized in the Third Battle of Vontor, Xim's final defeat. There are more pieces in those other crates. There were at least a thousand just like this one traveling onboard the *Queen of Ranroon* and guarding Xim's treasure when the ship vanished."

Han opened another crate. It contained a huge chestplate; Han knew he would never be able to uncrate the thing without Chewbacca's help. In the plate's center was Xim's insignia, a death's head with sunbursts in the eye sockets.

Bollux entered, chest panels open wide to let Blue Max perceive things as well. These two machines had been combined by a group of outlaw techs and had been instrumental in Han's survival at an Authority prison called Stars' End several adventures ago. Bollux and Max had elected to join Han and Chewbacca, exchanging labor for passage, in order to see the galaxy.

"Captain, First Mate Chewbacca says we'll be reverting to normal space shortly," the droid announced. Then his red photoreceptors fell on the cranial turret, and Han could have sworn they abruptly became brighter. In a voice more hurried than his usual drawl, Bollux queried, "Sir, what *is* that?" He went over to examine the thing more closely. Max studied the relic as well.

"So very old," mused the droid. "What machine is this?"

"War-robot," Han told him, sifting through the other crates. "Great-grandpa Bollux, maybe." He didn't notice the droid's metallic fingers quizzically feeling the shape of the massive head.

Han was mumbling to himself. "Reinforced stress points; heavy-gauge armor, all points. Look how thick it is! You could run a machine shop off those power-delivery systems. Hmm, and built-in weapons, chemical and energy both."

He stopped rummaging and looked at Skynx. "These things must've been unstoppable. Even with a blaster, I wouldn't want to mix with one." He slid the lid back on the crate. "Find yourselves a place and get comfortable, everybody. We'll revert from hyperspace as soon as I get to the cockpit. Where's Hasti? I can't hold up the whole—"

His jaw dropped. Hasti—it had to be her—had just swept into the forward compartment. But the factory-world, mining-camp girl was gone. The red hair now fell in soft, fine waves. She wore a costume of rich iridescent fabrics in black and crimson; the hem of her ruffled, wrapfront gown brushed the deckplates, and over it she wore a long quilted coat with voluminous sleeves, its formal cowl flung back and its gilt waist sash left open. Her steps revealed supple, ornamentally stitched buskins.

She had applied makeup, too, but with such restraint that Han couldn't tell what or how. She was cooler, more poised, and seemed older than Han recalled. Her expression dared him to make a crack. One side of him was trying to tally how long it had been since he had seen anyone this attractive.

"Girl," breathed Badure, "for a second there I thought you were a ghost. It might've been Lanni, standing there."

An hour ago I'd have said she couldn't find romance in a prison camp with a jetpack on! I'm slipping, Han thought. Then he found his voice. "But why?"

While Hasti inspected Han distantly, Badure explained. "When Lanni diverted course on a freight run to store the log-recorder disk at the vaults, she changed into this local outfit Hasti's wearing so word wouldn't leak that a woman from the mining camp had been there. Fortunately she gave us the rental code and retrieval combination before she was killed by J'uoch's people. Hasti must look as much like poor Lanni as possible, in case any of the vault personnel happen to remember her sister."

Hasti motioned back toward Han's quarters. "Nice wallow you have there; it looks like the end of a six-day sweepstakes party."

His reply was cut short by an angry caterwauling from the cockpit. It was Chewbacca insisting that Han come up for the reversion to normal space. "I wonder if I wouldn't be asking too much to view the procedure from the cockpit?" Skynx said to Han.

"Sure; we'll find some place for you." Han met Hasti's aloof gaze. "How about you? Care to watch?"

She pursed her mouth indifferently. Skynx left off observing what was, as far as he could conclude, a variation on human preening/courting rituals and excitedly hurried toward the cockpit, followed by Badure. Han, weighing Hasti's expression, decided neither to offer his arm nor to touch her in any ushering-along gesture.

None of them noticed Bollux, who remained behind, contemplating the war-robot's head, his cold fingers resting on the imposing armored brow.

☐ VI

DELLALT had, in its heyday, been a prominent member of a strategic cluster during the pre-Republic phase known locally as the Expansionist Period. That importance had run its course. Altering trade routes, increased ships' cruising ranges, intense commercial competition, social dislocation, and the realigning power centers of the emergent Republic—all had long since converted the planet to a seldom taken side trip, isolated even from the rest of the Tion Hegemony.

Dellalt's surface boasted far more water than soil. The treasure vaults of Xim were located near a lake on the southernmost of the planet's three continents, a hook-shaped piece of land that crossed Dellalt's equator and extended almost to its southern pole. Around the vaults stood Dellalt's single large population concentration, a small city built by Xim's engineers. The travelers studied it during their approach.

Heavy weapons emplacements and defensive structures around the city were now gutted ruins filled with crumbling machinery. Broken monorail pylons and once grand buildings, falling back to dust, were overgrown with thick dendroid vines. Recent construction was sparse, poorly planned, and done with crude materials. There was the wreckage of a sewage- and water-treatment plant, indicating just how far back Dellalt had slipped. Badure mentioned that the planet harbored a race of sauropteroids, large aquatic reptiles that lived in a rigidly codified truce with the human inhabitants.

Port officialdom was nonexistent; a bureaucracy would have been an unprofitable expense, something the Tion Hegemony avoided. Han and Badure, intending to attract attention, made a show of stretching and pacing as they came down the ramp to a landing area that was no more than a flat hilltop showing the scorches of former landings and liftoffs. Their breath crystallized in the cold air. Han had donned his own flight jacket. Glossy, cracked, and worn with age, it showed darker, unweathered spots where patches and insignia had been removed. He pulled his collar up against the wind.

Below them the decaying city spread out along slopes leading down to the long, narrow lake, part of Dellalt's intricate aquatic system. Han estimated from the condition of the landing area that it saw no more than three or four landings per Dellaltian year—probably just Tion patrol ships and the occasional marginal tramp trader. The planet's year was half again as long as a Standard one, with a shorter-than-Standard mean day. Gravity was slightly more than Standard, but since Han had adjusted the *Millennium Falcon*'s gravity during the flight, they scarcely noticed it now.

People came running up from the little city, laughing and making sounds of greeting. The women's attire was like Hasti's, with variations of color, layering, and cut. Male dress tended toward loose pantaloons, padded jackets, all manner of hats and turbans, and pleated, flowing cloaks and robes. Children copied their parents' appearance in miniature. All around these humans were packs of yipping, loping domestic animals, grainy-skinned quadrupeds with needlelike teeth and prehensile tails.

Han asked who owned the single building on the field, a decaying edifice of lockslab that might be used as warehouse or docking hangar. The owner appeared quickly, making his way through the mob with curses and insults that no one seemed to take personally. He was small but heavily built, and his scraggly whiskers failed to hide pockmarked cheeks and throat that had been ravaged by some local disease. His teeth were yellow-brown stumps. Crude or nonexistent medical care was too common on fringe worlds for Han to feel disgust anymore.

He inquired about the building. The language of

Dellalt was Standard, distorted with a thick accent. The man insisted that rental terms were so minor a problem that there was no reason to waste Han's time, that the outloading of cargo could begin at once. The pilot knew that to be a lie, but confrontation was a part of Badure's plan.

Bollux appeared and began making trips between the starship and the building. At first the perplexed droid found himself surrounded by screaming, laughing children and snarling, snapping domestic quadrupeds. But the cousins of the building's landlord threatened, cursed, and slapped them away, then formed an escort to see to it that the labor droid could work in relative peace. Still, many eyes followed the gleaming Bollux; such automata were unknown here. The landlord's cousins opened one of the building's doors just wide enough for the droid to enter and leave. He began stacking crates, canisters, pressure kegs, and boxes inside.

The crowd milled around and under the *Millennium Falcon*, timidly touching her landing gear and gawking up at her in amazement, yammering among themselves. Then someone noticed the Wookiee, who sat looking down from the cockpit. Shouts and shrieks went up; hands were thrust at the Wookiee in gestures meant to repel evil. Chewbacca gazed down on all the activity impassively, and Han wondered if it had occurred to any in the crowd that his first mate was manning the freighter's weaponry.

A considerable pile of cargo containers had already accumulated in the building when, with his cousins stationed around its main doors, the landlord abandoned his effusive welcomes and named an enormous rental fee. Badure shook his scarred fist under the landlord's nose, and Han shouted a threat. The landlord threw up his hands and besought his ancestors for justice, then insulted the offworlders' appearance and the circumstances of their birth. His cousins let the droid continue stacking cargo in his building, though.

Each time Bollux left the outbuilding, one of the cousins swung the door shut with a creak of primitive hinges. Waiting until she had heard that sound for the third time to be certain of the routine—and having timed the droid's purposely slow trips—Hasti pushed the lid off her shipping canister and stepped out, lifting her hem carefully and rubbing her cramped neck.

Anyone seen leaving the starship would have been trailed all over town by the crowds. That in turn would have made recovery of the log-recorder impossible. Badure's plan had circumvented all that.

The building had a small rear door. Everything was as Badure had predicted—on a backward world like Dellalt, the landlord could ill afford expensive locking systems on each door. Therefore, this rear door and the larger hanging door were secured from the inside, with only a smaller door set in the larger one equipped with a lockplate. Not that that mattered. Han Solo had given Hasti a vibrocutter in case she had needed to force her way out. But she needed merely to move the bolt and then emerged into the light behind the building, shouldering the door closed again.

Peering around the corner, she could isolate at least three different centers of furor. In one, Han Solo and Badure were squared off with the landlord, insulting one another's antecedents and personal hygiene in best Dellaltian haggling style; in another, people were pointing at and debating hotly over Chewbacca's origin; and finally, the landlord's cousins were battling the crowd so Bollux could keep filling the building with the containers they would later confiscate if the offworlders didn't meet the exorbitant rental fee. All the Dellaltians seemed quite happy with their unscheduled holiday.

At that juncture another distraction, also planned by Badure, occurred. Skynx ambled down the ramp, ostensibly to confer with Han and the old man. An astonished shout went up from the crowd, and most of the people tagging along after Bollux went at a run to see this new wonder.

Making sure her compact pistol was safe in an inner pocket, Hasti set off, keeping the building between herself and the field. She had draped the cowl over her head and went unnoticed. She had been in the city before, sent from the mining camp with Lanni to make minor purchases. Recalling the layout of the place, she set out for Xim's treasure vaults.

Pavement laid when the vaults were new had been chewed and disintegrated by use and time. The streets were rutted and hard-packed in the middle and muddy along the sides where slops had been dumped from overhanging windows. Hasti prudently kept along the middle way. Around her people ran, limped, or were carried toward the landing area. Two cadaverous old-sters, members of the local aristocracy, were carried past in an opulent sedan chair borne by six stooped bearers. A buckboard drawn by two skeletal, eight-legged dray beasts followed.

Three drunks lurched out of a drinking stall, arms around one another; they were waving ceramic tip-pling bowls in the air, sloshing liquor. They regarded her for a moment, then elbowed one another. Under the native code of ethics a woman was fairly safe, at least in town, but Hasti kept her eyes to the ground and her hand near her pistol. But the celebrants de-cided that the starship merited their attention first, or they would be excluded from an event the rest of the city would talk about all year.

Picking her way through a city that seemed to be falling apart before her eyes, Hasti at last came to the vaults of Xim the Despot. The vaults were contained within a sprawling, cameral complex of interlocking structures, immensely thick-walled and, in its day, im-pervious to forced entry. Still, thieves had gotten in over the years and, finding only empty vaults, yawn-ing treasure chambers, and waiting bins and unoc-cupied shelves, had soon departed. Only the occasional wanderer or scholar of the obscure came here to tour Xim's barren edifice now. The galaxy was rich in sights and marvels worth the seeing and easier to reach; there was little of allure in the haunted emptiness here.

In the vaults' worn and pitted façade were engraved Xim's insignia of the starburst-eyed death's head and characters from an ancient language: IN ETERNAL HOMAGE TO XIM, WHOSE FIST SHALL ENCLOSE THE STARS AND WHOSE NAME SHALL OUTLIVE TIME.

Hasti paused for a glimpse of herself in the gleaming stump of a fallen column, hoping she resembled her sister sufficiently. She fumed at the memory of Han Solo's sudden change of attitude toward her—first fussing over the buckling of her seatbelt and then his reckless—but expert—planetfall, done to impress her. Either the oaf couldn't see how much she disliked him or, more likely, refused to accept it.

At the top of the steps she crossed the wide, roofless portico and passed through the vaults' single, gigantic entranceway. The interior was cool and dark. There was a vast circular chamber under a dome half a kilometer in diameter, a mere vestibule to the huge vault complex.

But this outermost chamber was the only part of the vaults in use any more. Hasti's eyes adjusted to the light of weak glow-rods and tallow lanterns guttering smoke into the cavernous room designed to be lit by monumental illumi-panels. Farther in toward the center of the place was a small cluster of work tables, partitions, and cabinets—the administrative annex for the minor activity the vaults still housed.

A few Dellaltians, carrying data plaques, old-fashioned memo-wire spools, and even a few sheafs of paper computer-printout, passed by her. Hasti shook her head at the primitive operation. But, she remembered, the vaults had very few tenants. The Dellaltian Bank and Currency Exchange, a minor concern, was one, while the Landmark Preservation Office, charged with looking after the abandoned labyrinth with almost no resources, was that grouping of desks and partitions.

A man approached her from the semigloom—tall, broad-shouldered, his hair as white as his forked beard. He moved briskly; at his heels was an assistant, a smaller, grimmer man whose long black hair was parted down the middle and showed a white blaze.

The tall man's voice was hearty and charming. "I am steward of the vaults. How may I help you?"

Holding her chin high, Hasti answered in her best approximation of a local accent. "The lockboxes. I wish to recover my property."

The steward's hands circled one another, fingers gathered, in the Dellaltian sign of courtesy and invitation. "Of course; I shall assist you personally." He spoke to the other man, who departed.

Remembering to walk on his right, as a Dellaltian woman would, Hasti followed the steward. The vaults' corridors, musty with age, displayed mosaics of colored crystal so complicated that Hasti couldn't interpret them. Many of the pieces were cracked, and whole stretches were missing; they arched high overhead into shadow. Here, their footsteps resounded hollowly.

At last they came to a wall, not the end of the corridor but a partition of crudely cut stone that had plainly been mortared into place after the original construction. Set in the wall was a door that looked as if it had been scavenged from some later, less substantial building. Next to it was an audio pickup. The steward pointed to it.

"If the lady will speak into the voice-coder, we can proceed to the lockbox repository."

When Hasti's sister had told her and Badure about depositing the log-recorder disk she had told them the box-rental code and retrieval combination, but had mentioned no voice-coder. Hasti felt the pulse in her forehead and the thumping in her rib cage quicken.

The steward was waiting. Leaning to the audio pickup she said, as if in mystic invocation, "Lanni Troujow."

"My last offer," Badure threatened for the fourth time, resorting to hyperbole common on Dellalt, "is ten credits a day, guaranteed three-day minimum."

The landlord shrieked and tore hairs out of his beard, beat his chest with his free hand, and vowed to his ancestors that he would join them before letting plundering offworlders steal the food from his children's mouths. Skynx took it all in, amazed by the carefully measured affrontery of the hagglers.

Han listened with one ear, worried that Hasti might not have been able to get away from the landing area undetected. There was a tug at his shoulder; it was

Bollux. "I noticed this altercation, sir. Shall I continue to outload our cargo?"

That meant Hasti was away. Badure heard and understood. "Get everything back onboard until this son of contaminated genes, this landlord, bargains reasonably."

"Unthinkable!" screamed the landlord. "You have already made use of my precious building and diverted me from my other pursuits. A settlement must be made; I hereby hold your cargo against the arrival of the Fact-Finders." He and Badure swapped deadly oaths.

The landlord called the old man a horrible name. Skynx, quivering in excitement, immersed himself in the spirit of the thing, antennae trembling. "Devourer of eggs!"

Everyone stopped, glancing at the diminutive Ruurian, who swallowed, appalled at his rash outburst. The landlord departed, along with much of the crowd, hurling back epithets and leaving his cousins to guard the outbuilding. From somewhere, the cousins had produced bolt-operated slug rifles with hexagonal barrels and long, lens-type scopes.

Back onboard the *Falcon,* Badure threw himself into a chair. "That landlord! What a freighter bum he'd have made!"

Han grabbed Bollux. "What happened?"

"The men guarding the building entrance kept looking through the door after me as I deposited the cargo. It was some time before they became bored and gave all their attention over to Badure's performance and Skynx's appearance. Hasti was no longer in her crate, and the inner door was unbarred. At Blue Max's suggestion I resecured the door."

"Tell Maxie he's a good boy," Badure said. "I like you two; you've got a touch of larceny in you."

Bollux's chest plastron swung open, the halves coming apart like cabinet doors. Blue Max's photoreceptor lit up. "Thanks, Badure," he said, sounding smug. Han told himself, *I should keep an eye on that computer or he'll end up wearing juvie-gang colors and packing a vibro-shiv.*

Just at that moment, Skynx appeared with Chewbacca, who had just left the cockpit. The Wookiee was holding the metallic flask of vacuum-distilled jet juice the partners kept under the control console for special occasions. "Skynx," Badure said, "I think it's time to strike up the band."

Skynx flowed to the acceleration couch and on up into his nook. He began taking objects from his tree-like storage rack. "If you have no further tasks for us, sir," Bollux told Han, "Max and I would like to continue our study of Skynx's tapes."

"Whatever you want, old-timer."

Bollux crossed to the tech station, where he and the computer resumed their perusal of the ancient records Skynx had brought along. The labor droid, who had worked his way across the galaxy and had already outlived one body, possessed an almost sentient streak of curiosity, and Blue Max was always ready to absorb new information. The two mechanicals were particularly interested in technical data and other references to the giant war-robots of long-dead Xim.

Skynx, sitting up on his rearmost two sets of limbs, took and held a miniature amplified hammer-dulcimer in the next set and two hammers in each digital cluster of the next. He strapped a pair of tympanic pulsers around himself, tapping experimentally with the digits of his next-higher limbs. Above those he fastened a pair of small bellows to pump air to a horn held in his uppermost-but-one set of extremities. In the uppermost he took up a flute of sorts and tried a few runs. The sound was like the wind-cones Han remembered from his own homeworld. He wondered what kind of brain could coordinate all that activity.

Skynx launched into a merry air, full of sudden runs, bright interplay and humorous progressions, and impudent catches made to sound as if the instruments or Skynx's limbs were getting out of hand and taking their own course. The Ruurian made a great pretense of distress and bewilderment and a desperate effort to bring his extremities under control again. The others laughed, particularly Chewbacca, whose Wookiee chortles made the bulkheads ring. Badure rapped time

on the gameboard and even Han was tapping a toe or
two. He opened the flask, took a swig, and passed it
to the Wookiee. "Here, this'll put some curl in your
pelt." Chewbacca drank, then sent the flask along.
Even Skynx accepted a drink.

They demanded another number after that, and a
third. Badure eventually jumped up, both hands over
his head, to demonstrate the Bynarrian jig. He capered around the compartment as if he were twenty
kilos lighter and as many years younger.

At the height of the Bynarrian jig the ship's hatch
signaled. Badure and Chewbacca rushed off, eager to
see what Hasti had brought back. Bollux and Blue
Max looked up from the strobing rapid-readout screen,
and Skynx began extricating himself from his instruments.

"Step one completed!" he said in his quick fashion.
"Skynx, of the K'zagg Colony, off on a treasure hunt!
If my clutch-siblings could see me now!"

But when the Wookiee reentered the compartment,
he slumped dejectedly over to his partner and sank
into the couch, head in hairy hands. *Bad as that?*
thought Han. Badure followed, one arm clasped
around a despairing Hasti. She took a sip from the
flask, coughed, told her story quickly, then took another.

"Voice-coder?" Han exclaimed. "Nobody said anything about a voice-coder."

"Maybe Lanni never realized her voice was being
printed," Badure replied.

"That steward," Hasti muttered. "I should've jabbed
my gun into his bellybutton and offered to glaze his
gallstones for him."

Han handed the half-empty flask to his copilot and
rose. "Now we do it *my* way." He headed for the
cockpit, pulling on his flying gloves. Chewbacca fell
in behind. "Want to know how to make a withdrawal? Stick around."

Badure hurriedly interposed himself between the
two partners and the main passageway. "Steady
there, boys. Just what've you got in mind?"

Han grinned. "Swooping down on the vault, blowing the doors with the belly-turret guns, going in, and taking the disk. Don't bother getting up, folks; it'll all be over in a minute."

Badure shook his head. "What if a Tion patrol cruiser shows up? Or an Imperial ship? Would you care to have a hunter-killer team on your neck?"

Han made a move to step around him. "I'll chance it."

Hasti jumped up. "Well, I won't! Sit *down,* Solo! At least consider the options before you risk the death penalty for all of us."

Chewbacca awaited his friend's decision. Bollux watched impartially and Blue Max with a certain excitement.

"Some forethought might not be out of place here," Skynx contributed in a very subdued voice.

Han disliked complications and subterfuge, but his hasty action was stayed, for the moment, by the conviction that being dead was the least interesting thing in life. "All right, all right; who's hungry?" he asked. "I'm sick of ship's rations. Let's go see what kind of meal we can get in town. But if nobody thinks of a new one, my plan still goes." He clipped the flask to his gunbelt while Chewbacca gathered up his bowcaster and bandoleer of ammunition. Badure found the small purse of local currency he had brought, and Bollux shut his plastron halves on Blue Max.

Hasti saw Skynx shedding his instruments. "Hey, I never got to hear anything."

Badure looked around. "Bring them along," he bade Skynx. The Ruurian began tucking his instruments into carrying cinches he fastened around himself.

Pulling on his flight jacket, Han shut and sealed the hatch behind them. Storm clouds had moved in, and electrical discharges illuminated the clouds in strange flashes of red. Badure pointed out that the landlord's cousins had disappeared. "They probably figured out they were guarding empty boxes."

"More likely they didn't want to sit around in that leaky barn," Hasti reasoned. The rest of the onlookers who had been watching the starship from a distance, mostly children and the domestic yappers, were gone as well.

They set off downslope with Bollux bringing up the rear. Up this high, away from the docks, the streets were poorly maintained and lighting was unknown. They didn't get far.

Han was first to sense something wrong—everything was too quiet, too many ramshackle windows were shuttered. No lights were showing and no voices could be heard anywhere nearby. He grabbed Chewbacca's shoulder, and the bowcaster came up, the blaster appearing at the same time. By instinct, they stood back to back. Hasti had her mouth open to ask what was wrong when the spotlights hit them.

Han recognized them as hand-held spots and, figuring that a right-handed man would be holding the spot as far out with his left as he could, took an estimated aim.

"Don't!" a voice ordered. "We'll cut you all down if anyone fires a shot!"

They were surrounded. Han holstered his side arm, and the Wookiee lowered his bowcaster. Humans and various other beings appeared in the glare, waving rifles, riot guns, slug-shooters, and other weapons. Han and his companions were easily disarmed and their equipment examined. Skynx chittered in terror while their captors pawed his delicate musical instruments, but he was allowed to retain them.

Three individuals strode forward to search the captives. The smaller two were mainbreed human—twins, a young man and woman who shared traits of thick, straight brown hair and widow's peaks, startling black-irised eyes, and thin, intense, pale faces. The third personage hung back, a looming hulk in the light backwash of the spots. Han remembered the name Badure had mentioned: Egome Fass, the enforcer.

The twins approached them, the female in the lead. "J'uoch," murmured Hasti, shivering.

The twins' faces held the same rigid, lethal composure. "That's it," J'uoch replied quickly. "Where's the disk, Hasti? We know you went to the vaults."

She gave Han a chilly smile. Then the smile vanished and she turned again to Hasti. "Give it up, or we burn down your friends, starting with the pilot here."

Chewbacca's great arms tensed, fingers curling. He prepared to die as he would be expected to, head of a Wookiee Honor Family, his life so intimately intertwined with that of Han Solo that there existed no human word for the relationship.

Han, in turn, was choosing among several tactics, all of them suicidal, when Bollux spoke. "Captain Solo mustn't come to harm. I will open the *Millennium Falcon* for you."

The woman eyed him. It hadn't occurred to J'uoch that the droid would be cleared for ship access. "Very well. All we want is the log-recorder disk." Han, in the grip of adrenal overload, stared at Bollux and wondered what was going through the old labor droid's logic stacks. One fact did not escape him: he had heard high-pitched communication bursts exchanged between Bollux and Blue Max.

Their captors herded them back toward the *Falcon*. Too late, Han understood why the Dellaltians had scattered. He just hoped the two machines had a workable plan.

Bollux, climbing the ramp, was at the main hatch lock with several of J'uoch's people near. Strangely, just as the main hatch rolled up into its recess, the droid chose to swing his chest panels open. Then Han and the others heard Blue Max's high-speed burst signals.

An ear-splitting hiss of a hurtling object echoed through the air. One of the men who was guarding Bollux was lifted off his feet by terrific impact, and in the next moment was stretched headlong on the ramp. Another captor, farther down the ramp, was slammed in the shoulder and knocked through the air.

"Run for it!" Blue Max shrilled. As suddenly as that, chaos broke loose.

☐ VII

THE two strongarm specimens still standing at the top of the ramp ducked instinctively. Something small and fast swooshed past Han, knocking the humanoid who had been guarding him off his feet. Bollux pivoted to follow the action.

From the now-exposed Blue Max more high-pitched beeps issued forth. Han realized with some amazement that the computer module had managed to summon the remote target-globe from the *Falcon*'s interior and was using it as a weapon.

Before J'uoch's people could react, Han yelled, *"Hit 'em!"* He grabbed the nearest opponent's weapon, a slug-shooter carbine with a drum magazine and, twisting his leg behind the other's, toppled him over.

Badure rammed his elbow back into the face of his guard and turned to grapple with him. Chewbacca was less fortunate. Preparing to enter the fray, he was unaware that the massive Egome Fass had stolen up behind him. The enforcer's hard fist crashed into the base of the Wookiee's skull.

Chewbacca staggered, nearly falling to his knees, but his tremendous strength bore him up again. He turned groggily to give battle, but Egome Fass's first blow had given the enforcer a formidable edge. He avoided Chewbacca's slowed counterpunch and landed another blow, bringing his fist down on the Wookiee's shoulder. And this time the *Falcon*'s first mate went down.

Badure was having a difficult time with his second guard, who was young and fast. They struggled, feet shuffling in the dry dust, but just as the older man was gaining the upper hand by dint of weight and reach, he was tackled low around the knees and went down.

The tackler was Hasti. She had seen that J'uoch's men on the ramp were about to open fire on Badure. Propelled by its repulsor power and forced air, the remote globe had taken two more antagonists out of the fight. J'uoch was shooting at it with Hasti's confiscated pistol, missing, and screaming orders that her troops ignored.

Han had retrieved the carbine, knocking his opponent away with a stroke of the weapon's butt. He spotted his partner struggling to rise as Egome Fass hovered over him. The enforcer's hood was thrown back, and in the light spilling down through the hatch, Han saw the humanoid's huge, square jaw and tiny, gleaming eyes set far back under thick, bony ridges of brow.

Han clamped the carbine stock to his hip and squeezed off a burst. The weapon stuttered with a deafening staccato and reeked of burned propellant. A stream of slugs plucked at the enforcer's chest but only ripped away fragments of cloth. Egome Fass was wearing body armor under his outsized coveralls. Before Han could adjust for effect, the humanoid lunged for cover.

A wash of white fire flared on Han's right. Turning, he saw that it was a power-pistol shot aimed at Badure by a man on the ramp who missed because Hasti had just tackled the old man. But it hit the man with whom Badure had been struggling. He shrieked once and died as he fell.

Han grabbed Chewbacca's elbow as the Wookiee struggled to his feet, shaking his head to clear it. Retaking the *Falcon* was impossible; the two remaining guards at the ramp head were kneeling in the shelter of the hatchway and firing into the night. "Get back!" Han hollered to his companions. He moved back, firing in brief bursts, followed by Hasti and Badure with Skynx scuttling rapidly behind.

The spotty return fire, hasty and poorly aimed, never came close. But one guard, a leather-skinned creature with a horny carapace, blocked Bollux's retreat. Blue Max beeped, and immediately the remote flashed out of the darkness, striking the creature from behind and knocking it over. Since the remote couldn't operate at any great distance from the starship, Max gave the signal that sent it jetting back onboard.

The labor droid hurried after the others, bounding in long strides made possible by heavy-duty suspension. The group ran, bounded, and scuttled to the edge of the landing area. All the while Han raked the field behind them to keep J'uoch's people pinned down. Then the carbine went silent.

"Drum's empty," he said. Off in the night he could hear J'uoch railing at her followers and calling for a comlink.

"She's posting a guard on the ship and calling for reinforcements," Badure announced. "We'd best lose ourselves in town for a while."

The group descended through the city in an informal race, past shuttered shops and locked doors. No lights could be seen; the Dellaltians who had seemed so curious earlier wanted no part of this lethal dispute among offworlders. Leading the others, Han plunged into an alley, followed it to a market plaza, and hurried down a trellised side street that smelled of strange foods and fuels.

They came to a factory district. Pausing in the shadows, the humans and the Wookiee leaned against a wall and fought for breath while Bollux waited impassively and Skynx, with a superior respiratory system, checked his carrier cinches to make sure that none of his precious instruments had been damaged.

"You should've snagged a gun," Han puffed, "instead of worrying about that one-man band of yours."

"These have been making music in my family for a dozen generations," Skynx replied indignantly. "And I'm sure I don't know how I could've wrested a weapon away from some malodorous ruffian four times my size."

Han gave up the argument and checked the nearby rooftops. "Can anybody spot a ladder or staircase? We have to see if they're trailing us."

"Now I can be of help there, I believe," Skynx announced. A nearby pole supported fiber-optic cables for in-town communications; wrapping himself around it, Skynx spiraled up the pole, protecting his instruments carefully. Since all the buildings were one-story affairs, he had a good view of the surrounding area.

Having reconnoitered, Skynx corkscrewed his way down the pole again. "There are search parties working their way down through town," he told them. "They have hand-held spotlights; I assume them to be using comlinks." He tried to hide his fearful quaking.

"Did you see their ship?" Han asked eagerly. "It must be around here somewhere. Perhaps we could pick up some fire power there."

But Skynx hadn't spotted it. They decided to try to skirt the search parties' pattern and see if they couldn't get back to the *Millennium Falcon*. Skynx's feathery antennae wavered in the air, attentive to vibrations. "Captain, I hear something."

They all held their breath and listened. A rumbling swelled until it shook the ground. "Looks like J'uoch got through on the comlink," observed Badure over the tumult. An enormous vessel mounted with heavy guns was hovering above the landing area, its flood-lights playing over the city. The fugitives pressed back into the shadows.

The ponderous lighter couldn't hover and search for long; instead she descended. "There'll be more manpower onboard her," Badure warned. "Skynx, shinny up and take a look. Be careful."

The Ruurian went up a nearby line-pole and was down again almost at once. "The big ship must have dropped off parties down in the lakeside area," he told them urgently. "I saw them spreading out, coming up the hill. And there's a group of three coming down this way from above. One of them is carrying Chewbacca's bowcaster."

The Wookiee growled ominously. Han agreed, "Let's take care of them, but *good*." No one mentioned surrender; it was plain J'uoch would do anything to get what she wanted.

The search party flashed hand-held spots into alleys and doorways. Teams were being organized

to scour the rooftops; virtually every trustworthy being who could be spared from the mining camp had
been armed and brought to the scene.

The man leading this particular party, the man
whose carbine Han had appropriated, carried Chewbacca's bowcaster and had tucked Han's blaster into
his belt. He had seen a Wookiee bowcaster used in
the holo-thrillers and was determined to get even
with the two by downing them with their own weapons. He was delighted, therefore, to see a looming,
shaggy shape step out of the darkness before him.

Blocking his companions in the process, the man
with the bowcaster took a stance and fired. But Chewbacca ducked at the last instant, knowing that the
man's unfamiliarity with the feel and aiming charac-
teristics of the bowcaster would cause a first-round
miss. In a flash the Wookiee hurled himself forward.

The man gave the bowcaster's foregrip a yank to
recock it and strip another round off the magazine for
a second shot. But he got nowhere; the weapon's
mechanism was set for a Wookiee's brawn and length
of arm. Before he could cast it aside and pull out
Han's blaster, a mountain of angry brown fur descended upon him.

The other two searchers fanned out to either side.
One was felled immediately as Han Solo stepped out
of the shadows and knocked him out with a swipe of
the carbine's butt. The other was stunned by masonry
brickbats flung by Hasti and Badure.

Han adroitly snatched his victim's pistol and fired
at the brickbat-stunned searcher. Yelling, the man
clenched his calf and fell. Meanwhile Chewbacca
had separated his man from the bowcaster and thrown
him against a wall. The man crashed with an impressive thud and slid to the ground.

"You'll live," Han decided, toeing over the man
he had shot and waving his recaptured blaster, "*if*
you make some worthwhile conversation. How many
guards on my ship?"

The man licked his fear-parched lips. "Ten, maybe
twelve. A few actually onboard, the rest around her."

"What about the ship you came in?" Hasti asked their captive. "The first one, not that big lighter."

Han slightly depressed the blaster trigger.

The man gasped. "Backslope of town, below the landing area, in the rocks."

Badure came up, having collected the comlink dropped by the bowcaster thief. "Sonny boy, you just bought yourself a future." Then he told them that J'uoch's spaceboat was grounded on an expanse of flat stone, with only two men guarding her. "I've grown to dislike unnecessary killing," Badure explained, setting an appropriated stun-gun for maximum dispersal. He squeezed the trigger, and blue rings of energy leaped outward. Immediately the two guards collapsed. Badure and Hasti patted them down for whatever weapons or equipment they might have, then Han climbed into the boat and moved to the pilot's seat. "Fueled and ready!"

Chewbacca, examining the copilot's side of the board, woofed a question.

"No. We won't leave Dellalt without the *Falcon;* we couldn't get out of the system with this baby carriage anyway," Han replied. "We'll jump out of their search locus, then work out our next move." He began throwing switches and punching instructions into the flight computer.

A warning sounded and the board lit up. Chewbacca threw his head back and yeowled his frustration. From the console rang J'uoch's voice: "Attention, landing boat, attention! Why are you attempting to violate instrument lock? Guard detail, answer!"

"I need tools; they've got the board locked down," Han said urgently. Chewbacca dug long fingers around the edges of the utility locker's door and ripped it away. Han was busy unfastening the console's housing latches. The Wookiee grabbed some implements from the locker and handed them to Han, and soon the partners were attacking the lockdown mechanism, ignoring J'uoch's vehement transmissions that crackled in the background.

Chewbacca howled in triumph, neutralizing one security circuit. "Got the other," Han crowed. But

their elation disappeared as they heard the thunder
of mass-lift thrusters.

"She's coming after us in the lighter!" Hasti yelled
from the hatchway. "How soon can we lift off?"

"She's too close with those heavy cannons," Han
rasped. "But at least we'll have a diversion. Get
clear!"

The others ran for it. There was a chart readout
on the console; Han slipped it into his vest and,
with one foot out the hatch, inserted a series of instructions into the console. Automatic sequence cycled
the hatch shut, and the boat lifted off.

Han hurdled a rock and crouched in its shelter
with the others, and they watched the spaceboat rise
into the night sky. The lighter was already on a close
interception course; it seemed to Han a good time to
get as far as possible from the liftoff site. Having distracted those on the lighter, the fugitives moved off in
a ragged line. Chewbacca kept rearguard and, wield-
ing a clump of dry red shrubbery, eradicated the
few prints they'd left on the rocky terrain.

The spaceboat picked up speed, following Han's
programming. The lighter's heavy artillery spoke,
and tremendous spears of green-white energy made a
brief noon in the Dellaltian night. The first salvo
missed but gave the gunners their registration. The
second hit dead center, several beams converging
on the small boat at once. It exploded in a fireball,
leaving a few scraps of burning wreckage to flutter
from the sky.

"Capturing us wasn't such a big priority after all,"
Badure observed.

They had barely reached the temporary shelter of
a rocky outcropping and hidden themselves among the
boulders when the lighter returned with a rumble of
brute thrusters and settled in where the boat had lifted.
In moments the area was swarming with armed
searchers sweeping hand-held spots. The stunned
guards were quickly discovered, the ground examined.

"They're buying it!" Hasti whispered with muted
elation. The searchers noted the prints left by Han and
the others when they had approached the boat but

missed any sign of departure, thanks to Chewbacca's painstaking work. The dozing guards were lugged aboard the lighter and the rest of J'uoch's employees embarked. Thrusters flared again.

Han's mind was racing. Now that they were armed and J'uoch apparently believed them dead, they had a chance of retaking the *Millennium Falcon*. Han expected to see the lighter land next to his own ship, to take away the guards onboard. Instead, the larger vessel hovered above the freighter. The *Falcon*'s ramp was up, her ramp-bay doors closed. Han suddenly understood what was happening.

He threw himself forward at a flat-out run, bellowing at the top of his lungs, with Chewbacca only a step behind. No one on either ship heard them, of course; the lighter, its hoisting gear making loud contact with the freighter's upper hull and achieving tractor-lock on the smaller ship, lowered her mechanical support booms. In the same manner as she transported mining equipment, the lighter lifted off with the *Millennium Falcon* tucked up tightly to her underside.

The lighter veered south, gathering speed and altitude as she went. Han slowed to a stop. In despair he and Chewbacca watched their ship being borne away across the lake and over the mountains beyond. The others caught up.

"They think the log-recorder disk is onboard, isn't that it, Captain?" Skynx asked, somewhat in shock. "They searched us and didn't find it and tried to kill us, so they must assume we left it onboard the *Falcon*."

"Where are they headed?" Han asked tonelessly.

"Straight for the mining camp," Badure answered. "They'll have all the time and privacy they need to tear—to search her thoroughly."

Han pivoted on his heel and walked off toward town. A drizzle was starting.

"Where are you going? Where are *we* going?" Skynx yelped as the others hurried after.

"I want my ship back," said Han simply.

☐ VIII

"IT'S a lamebrained scheme, even for you," Hasti was saying. Han peered into the grayness and wished Badure would return.

The drizzle had become a freezing-cold downpour during the night, then slackened to a drizzle again. Han and the others, awaiting the old man, had taken shelter under a tarp behind piles of cargo in a broad-eaved wooden warehouse by the docks. They were sipping sparingly from the flask, which had remained clipped to Han's gunbelt throughout the night's action.

They were damp, bedraggled, and miserable. Han's hair was plastered flat against his skull, as was Hasti's. Drops fell from Skynx's matted wool, and Chewbacca's pelt had started exuding the peculiar odor of a wet Wookiee. Han reached out and patted his friend's head in a gesture of consolation, wishing there were something he could do for Bollux and Max. The two automata, abiding patiently, were worried that their moisture-proofing would fail.

"You haven't got a prayer of pulling this off, Solo," the girl finished.

He swiped a damp strand of hair off his forehead. "Then don't come along. There'll be another ship through here any year now."

A man in a shabby cloak appeared, splashing through the puddles, bearing a bundle on his shoulder. Han, his blaster's scope set for night shooting, identified Badure. The old man crouched with them under the tarp. Having acquired a cloak from an alley-sleeper, he had contrived to buy four more. Han and Hasti found that two fit them passably well and even Bollux could don one stiffly, unaccustomed as he was to the extraordinary feel of clothing. But the biggest cloak Badure had brought could barely contain Chewbacca; though its hood managed to cover his face from casual observation, his shaggy arms and legs stuck out.

"Maybe we could wrap him in bunting, like mittens and leggings," Badure suggested, then turned to Skynx. "I didn't forget you, my dear Professor." With a flourish he produced a shoulder bag, which he held open invitingly.

Skynx shrank back, antennae wobbling in dismay. "Surely you can't mean. . . . This is unacceptable!"

"Just until we're out of town," Han coaxed.

"Um, about that, son," Badure said, "maybe we should lie low awhile instead."

"Do what you feel like; this could be a bad hike. But they're probably tearing the *Falcon* apart at that mining camp."

"Then what's the point in going?" Hasti remonstrated. "It's a couple of hundred kilometers. Your ship'll be in pieces."

"Then I'll put her back together again!" he near-hollered, then calmed. "Besides, how did J'uoch and company show up so fast, unless she's got contacts here? We'd be sitting targets, not even to mention the average citizen's dislike of offworlders. We could end up bunking in the local slams."

Badure looked resigned. "Then it's the Heel-and-Toe Express for us."

The rain was letting up, the sky lightening. Han studied the chart readout he had picked up. It turned out to contain a complete survey map of the planet, dated but in exacting detail. "At least we had the good luck to get this."

Hasti sniffed. "You spacers and mariners and aviators are all alike: no religion, but plenty of superstition. Always ready to invoke luck."

To forestall another verbal skirmish, Badure jumped in. "The first thing is to get across the lake; there are no connections south on this side. No air service anywhere, but there's some ground transport over there somewhere. The only way across is a ferry service run by the natives, the Swimmers. They're jealous of their territory and they charge a fee."

Han wasn't sure he wanted to be transported by one of the sauropteroids, the Swimming People of Dellalt. "We could hike around the lake," he proposed.

"It would take us five or six extra days unless we could negotiate a vehicle or get our hands on some riding animals."

"Let's check the ferry. What about food and equipment?"

Badure looked askance. "What about lovely ladies and hot food? There'll be settlements along the way; we'll have to improvise." He blew his breath out, and it crystallized.

"Are you coming or staying?" Han asked Hasti.

She gave him a scalding glare. "Why bother asking? You'll lean on people until there's no choice left."

The moderately safe and comfortable adventure envisioned by Skynx had become a very real struggle for survival, but his Ruurian practicality made his decision simple. "I believe I'll remain with you, Captain," he said. Han almost laughed, but Skynx's simple tone of pragmatism and self-preservation lifted his opinion of the Ruurian a notch.

"Glad to have you. All right; down to the docks and across the lake."

Skynx crawled unwillingly into the bag, which Chewbacca then shouldered. They proceeded in a tight group, with Badure in the lead and Hasti and Han on the flanks. The Wookiee and Bollux kept to the middle of the group in hopes that in the poor light and rain they would be mistaken for humans, one extremely tall, the other barrel-chested.

Skynx poked his head out of the bag, feathery antennae thrashing. "Captain, it smells awful in here, and it's cramped." Han pushed him back down, then as an afterthought gave him the flask.

The docks and their moored embarkation floats were already busy. Leaving the others in the partial concealment of stacks of cargo, Han and Badure went to inquire about passage.

Though the docks had space for many of the tow-

rafts used by Dellalt's native sauropteroids, only the
middle area seemed busy. Then, scanning the scene,
Han saw one lonely raft off to the right. Though
Badure had briefly described the Swimmers, Han still
found them a startling sight.

Men were loading cargo aboard the tow-rafts, which
were tied at the embarkation floats. Tow-lines and
harnesses bobbed as the rafts waited in the water. Beyond them lazed twenty or so sauropteroids, circling
or treading water with flipper strokes of immense
power. They ranged from ten to fifteen meters in
length, their heads held high from the water on long
muscular necks as they moved in the lake. Their hides
varied from a light gray to a deep green-black; lacking
nostrils, they had blowholes at the tops of their long
skulls. They idled, waiting for the men ashore to complete the manual labor.

One of the men, a burly individual with a jeweled
ring in one ear and bits of food and droplets of break-
fast nectar in his beard, was checking cargo against
a manifest. As Badure explined their needs, he listened, playing with his stylus.

"You will have to talk money with the Top Bull," he
informed them with a smirk Han didn't like, then
called out: "Ho, Kasarax! Two seeking passage here!"
He returned to his work as if the two men no longer
existed.

Han and Badure went to the dock's edge and
stepped onto an embarkation float. A sauropteroid approached with a few beats of his flippers. Han surreptitiously moved his hand closer to his concealed
blaster. He was ill at ease at seeing Kasarax's size and
his hard, narrow head with its fangs longer than a
man's forearm.

Kasarax trod water next to the float. When he
spoke, the blast of sound and fishy breath made both
men fall back a bit. His pronunciation was distorted
but intelligible. "Passage is forty *driit*," the creature
announced, a hefty sum in Dellaltian currency, *"each.
And don't bother haggling; we don't fancy that down
here at the docks."* Kasarax blew a spout of con-

densing moisture out the blowhole in his head to punctuate the statement.

"What about the others?" Han murmured to Badure, indicating the rest of the sauropteroid pack.

But Kasarax caught Han's query and hissed like a pressure valve. "They do as I say! And I say you cross for forty *driit!*" He feinted, as if he were going to strike, a snakish movement that rocked the float with turbulence. Han and Badure scrambled onto the dock as the men there guffawed.

The man with the manifest approached. "I'm chief of Kasarax's shore gang; you may pay me."

Han, red in the face, was growing more furious by the moment at this high-handed treatment. But Badure, glancing toward the lone raft they had noticed earlier, asked, "What about him?"

A lone Swimmer was down there, a big, battle-torn old bull, watching events silently. The shore-gang chief forgot his laughter. "If you enjoy living, ignore him. Only Kasarax's pack plies this part of the lake!"

Still fuming, Han strode down the dock. Badure followed after a moment's indecision. The shore-gang chief called, "I give you fair warning, strangers!"

The old bull reared up a bit as they approached. He was the size of Kasarax, his hide a near-black, networked with scars. His left eye was gone, lost in a long-ago battle, and his flippers were notched and bitten. But when he opened his mouth his tremendous fangs gleamed like honed weapons. "You're new faces to the docks," he said in a whistling voice.

"We want to get across the lake," Han began. "But we can't meet Kasarax's price."

"Once, human, I'd have towed you across as quickly as you please and carefully, too, for eight *driit* each." Han was about to accept when the creature cut him off. "But today I tow for free."

"Why?" Han and Badure asked together.

The bull made a burbling sound that they took to be a laugh, and shot a blast from his blowhole. "I, Shazeen, have vowed to show Kasarax that any of the Swimming People are free to work this dock, like any other. But I need passengers, and Kasarax's shore gang keeps those away."

The shore gang was gathered in conference, grouped in a knot of perhaps twenty, and shooting murderous looks at Han, Badure, and Shazeen. "Can you meet us somewhere farther down the shore?" Han asked the native Dellaltian.

Shazeen reared, water streaming from his black back, looking like some primitive's war god. "Boarding here at the dock is the whole point! Do that and I will do the rest, nor will any of the Swimming People meddle with you; it's Shazeen they must deal with, that is our Law, which not even Kasarax dares ignore!"

Badure pulled thoughtfully at his lower lip. "We might go around the lake."

Han shook his head. "In how many days?" He turned to Shazeen. "There are a couple more passengers. We'll be right back."

"If they menace you on the docks, I cannot interfere," Shazeen warned. "That is the Law. But they won't dare use weapons unless you do for fear the other humans, the ones who've been driven from their jobs, will have cause to intercede."

Badure clapped Han's shoulder. "I could stand a little cruise right now, Slick." Han gave him a wicked grin; they started back.

The others were standing where they had been left. Hasti held a large cone of plasform that contained a mass of lumpy, pasty dough, which she and Chewbacca were eating with their fingers. She offered some to Badure and Han. "We were starving; I picked this up from a vendor. What's the plan?"

Badure explained as they shared the doughy stuff. It was thick and gluey but had a pleasing flavor, like nutmeat. "So," finished Han, "no shooting unless we have to. How's Skynx?"

The Wookiee chortled and held open the shoulder bag. The Ruurian lay in a near-circle, clutching the flask. When he saw Han, his faceted red eyes, which were somewhat glazed, grew wider. Skynx hiccupped, then chirped, "You old pirate! Where've you been?"

He flicked an antenna across Han's nose, then collapsed in chittering laughter.

"Oh, great," said Han, "he's tight as a scalp tick." Han tried to recapture the flask, but Skynx curled into a ball and was gripping it with four limb-sets.

"He said he's never metabolized that much ethanol before," said Hasti, looking slightly amused. "That's exactly how he said it."

"Keep it then," Han told Skynx. "But stay down; we're going for a ride."

Skynx's muffled voice came from the shoulder bag, "Perfect idea!"

They made their way back to the dock. Men from Kasarax's shore gang blocked their way to the embarkation float. Others, not of the gang, had appeared and leaned against walls or stacked cargo, carrying spring-guns, firearms, and makeshift weapons. Han remembered what Shazeen had said: these people had been forced out of a living by Kasarax's racket. None had been willing to risk riding with Shazeen, but they would see to it no weapons were used to keep Han's party from doing so. The rest of the shore gang was scattered around the docks, holding weapons of their own. As Han understood it, any shooting would trigger a general bloodbath, but anything short of that was allowable.

When Han was within a few paces, the shore-gang chief addressed him. "That's close enough." Several of his men were whispering among themselves, seeing the size of the cloaked and hooded Chewbacca.

Han moved closer, giving out a string of bland cordialities. He had the impression that the man was a good brawler and thought: Victory first; questions later! The chief reached to shove him back, with a warning. "I'm not telling you again, stranger!"

How right, agreed Han silently. He speedrew, blindingly fast, and placed his gun against the chief's head. The man was shoving and warning one instant, falling the next, with a look of surprise on his face. Han had time to backhand another man and give the shore-gang chief a stiff shove, such was the surprise he had generated. Then he had to duck a truncheon, and the scene erupted.

One young shore-gang member swung an eager one-two combination at Bollux, a short set-up jab and a long uppercut that would have done considerable damage to a human. But the youth's fist gonged off the droid's hard midsection and rebounded from his reinforced faceplate. As the boy cried out in agony, Hasti stepped around Bollux and brought the barrel of her gun down on his head.

Another shore-gangster reached for Han, who was otherwise occupied. So Badure stopped him with a forearm block and lashed out with his foot, kicking high and hard. His antagonist dropped. They had done well enough for the moment, but now the rest of the shore-gangsters pressed in vengefully.

Then Chewbacca joined the brawl.

The Wookiee had stepped back to shuck the shoulder bag and put Skynx out of danger and to lay down his bowcaster. His hood still pulled low, he selected two men, shook them hard, then hurled them up and back in either direction. A swing of one long arm brushed another man back off the dock; Chewbacca kicked out in the opposite direction, connecting with a man who had lunged at Hasti. The man flew sideways, tumbled twice, and stretched out full length on the dock.

Two men tackled the Wookiee from either side. He ignored them, his legs as sturdy as columns beneath him. He struck out all around him, felling opponents with each blow.

The fight raged around Chewbacca, a flock of flailing, desperate shore-gangsters swarming at him. Spoiling for a fight since he had been downed by Egome Fass's treacherous attack, the Wookiee obliged them. Bodies flew back, up, over. The *Millennium Falcon*'s first mate restrained himself to spare needless bloodshed. His companions found themselves left out of the riot with only occasional assistance to be rendered in the form of a tap on the head, a shove, or a shouted warning.

Chewbacca found time to give each of his legs a

shake, and the men straining at them were flung
loose. Those who remained standing made a con-
certed charge. The Wookiee spread his arms, scooped
up all three of them, and dashed them against the
dock. One of them, the gang chief, who had recovered
from Han's blow and reentered the fight, pulled a
punch-dagger from a forearm sheath.

Han angled for a clear shot then, whatever the con-
sequences. But Chewbacca caught the chief's movement. The Wookiee's head snapped around, his hood
falling back for the first time, and he unleashed a full-
throated roar into the shore-gang chief's face, drawing
his lips back off his jutting fangs. The chief turned
absolutely white, eyes bulging, and managed to produce the smallest of squeaks. His punch-dagger fell
from limp fingers. The snarling Wookiee, having at-
tended to all the others, set the man down and put
one forefinger against his chest. The chief fell backward to the deck, trying to draw breath.

Hasti grabbed Chewbacca's bowcaster and her
dropped cone of dough; Badure held the sack containing Skynx, from which emerged chitters of hilarity.
Han grabbed his partner's arm. "Gangplank's going
up!"

They dashed for the embarkation float, hopping
one by one to the tow-raft. Shazeen, who had watched
the whole encounter, loosed a blast from his blowhole.
Closing a nictitating membrane over his eye, he
ducked beneath the water to reemerge with his head
through the tow harness, commanding, "Cast off!"
Badure, last in line, brought the raft's painter with
him.

They had expected Shazeen to move off quickly,
but the Swimmer warped the raft out slowly. When
he had put a few dozen meters between the raft and
the dock, he slipped the tow harness by submerging,
then resurfaced to nudge it to a stop with his rocklike
snout. "That was some fine thumping!" he hailed.
Throwing his head back, he issued an oscillating call
that rolled across the water. "Shazeen salutes you,"
he clarified.

"Uh, thanks," Han replied dubiously. "What's the holdup?"

"We wait for Kasarax," Shazeen answered serenely.

Han's outburst was forestalled when another sauropteroid surfaced next to Shazeen, whistling and hissing with mouth and blowhole. "Use their language, woman," Shazeen chided the newcomer, who was smaller and lighter of hide but nearly as battle-scarred as the big bull. "These are Shazeen's friends. That pipsqueak there with the hairy face can really *thump,* can't he?"

The female switched to Standard. "Will you really oppose Kasarax?"

"No one tells Shazeen where he may or may not swim," replied the other creature.

"Then the rest of us are behind you!" she answered. "We'll keep Kasarax's followers out of it." The lake water swirled as it closed over her head.

"Drop anchor!" shouted Han. "Cut the power! Cancel the reservations! You never said anything about a faceoff."

"A race, a mere formality," assured Shazeen. "Kasarax must pretend now that it's a right-of-way dispute, to conform with the Law."

"*If* he can get passengers," Hasti broke in. "Look!"

Kasarax was having trouble getting any of his shore gang aboard his tow-raft. The clash at the dock had put doubt in them; now they were having second thoughts about being dragged into the middle of a Swimmer dispute. Their chief, too, hesitated.

Kasarax lost his temper and thrashed himself up over his tow-raft, half onto the dock. Men drew back from the enormous bulk and the steaming, gaping mouth. Kasarax bent down at the chief.

"You'll do as I say! There's nowhere you can hide from me, even in that shelter you built under your house. If you make me, I'll dig you out like a stoneshell from the lake bottom. And the whole time, *you'll hear me coming!*"

The shore-gang chief's nerve broke. White-faced, he scurried aboard the tow-raft, pulling along several unwilling followers and browbeating several others to accompany him.

"Mighty persuasive lad, that nephew of mine," reflected Shazeen.

"Nephew?" Hasti burst out.

"That's right. For years and years I whipped every challenger who came along, but I finally got tired of being Top Bull. I drifted north, where it's warm and the fish are fat and tasty. Kasarax has been running wild too long; partly my fault. I think shore folks put this takeover nonsense into his head, though."

"Another victory for progress," Badure murmured. Kasarax was nudging his tow-raft up even with Shazeen's.

"Anyway, don't worry," Shazeen told them. "The Swimming People won't attack you, so don't use your weapons on them, or you turn it into a death-matter. That's the Law."

"What about the other humans?" Han called, but too late; Shazeen had gone to confront Kasarax. The shore-gang members had brought along their harpoon spring-guns and a variety of dockside cutlery.

The two bulls churned the water, trumpeting to one another. At length Shazeen switched to human speech. "Stay clear of my course!"

"And you from mine!" Kasarax retorted. They both plunged for their tow-rafts, flippers beating with full force, diving for their harnesses and creating rolling swells. They reemerged with heads through harnesses and snapped the towing hawsers taut. The hawsers creaked with the strain, wringing the water from them. Water gushed up from the rafts' blunt bows, breaking in spray and foam. Everyone on both rafts fell to the deck, snatching frantically for a handhold.

Kasarax and Shazeen breasted the water neck and neck, shrilling challenges to one another. Han began to wonder whether a hike around the lake wouldn't have been a better idea after all. *Why do I always think of these things too late?*

☐ IX

TOWING hawsers thrummed like bowstrings. The rafts moved forward with surges matching the Swimmers' rhythms.

Han clasped the low deck rail. The water teemed with sauropteroids, both Kasarax's cronies and Shazeen's supporters, who had been kept from work by Kasarax's alliance with the shore gang.

Long, scaled necks cut the water; rolling backs and broad flippers showed with each dive, and the spray of swimming and blasting blowholes made it seem the rain had resumed.

"Chewie!" shouted Hasti, who was hugging a rail stanchion, "the bag!"

The shoulder bag containing Skynx was sliding aft. Badure rolled from a stern-rail corner and caught it, wrapping his legs around a stanchion. Skynx popped out of the bag, his big red eyes more glazed now than before.

Taking in their situation unsteadily, the Ruurian scuttled up halfway onto Badure's head, his antennae bending in the breeze, clinging resolutely with every digit he could spare, and hurled the empty jet-juice flask into the air, cheering, *"Weee-ee heee-ee!* I bet five *driit* on us!" Spying Kasarax's raft, he added shrewdly, "And five more on them!" He sank back down into the bag, which Badure closed over him.

The rough ride didn't trouble Han nearly as much as the fact that this was no ordinary race. The two bulls were straining, neither able to gain headway against the other. Kasarax made a bid for the lead, then another, but Shazeen matched his spurts and held the pace. Han could hear their booming grunts of effort over the rush of the wind and the slapping of water against the rafts.

Kasarax changed tactics, slackening his line. Shazeen followed suit. The younger creature changed course in an instant, cutting across Shazeen's path just behind his elder. He ducked under Shazeen's towing hawsers and pulled hard. His tow-raft came slashing after, hawsers brushing at angles under Shazeen's.

Han saw the shore-gang chief hoist a broad-bladed axe; Kasarax's men obviously intended to sever Shazeen's hawsers when the hawsers came up against Kasarax's raft's bow rail. The pilot drew without thinking; a blaster bolt flickered red across the water, and the axehead jolted, sparks arcing from it, a black-edged hole burned through it. The shore-gang chief dropped it with a cry as his men ducked.

Someone else grabbed the axe and swung it as both rafts and the Swimmers towing them were dragged and slewed around by each other's momentum. Han's aim was spoiled and the axehead descended. Perhaps it was an off-world product with an enhanced edge; in any case the axe parted a hawser with one blow and bit into the bow rail. Shazeen's raft swung, coming nearly side-on, with the unbalanced pull of the remaining hawser.

The chief had the axe back, ready to chop the other hawser. Han was aiming carefully at the axe when Shazeen changed course in an effort to see what had happened. The remaining towing hawser dragged across Kasarax's raft's rail, catching the shore-gang chief and pulling him overboard. At the same moment Shazeen's maneuver bumped his own raft into a trough. Han lost his footing, slipped, and fell, whereupon the blaster flew from his hand.

The chief was still clinging to Shazeen's remaining tow-hawser, lower body in the water, sawing at it with a knife. Han couldn't spot his blaster, but was determined not to let that second line be severed. The gang chief was working at the hawser, Hasti was shouting something about not starting a firefight, and Badure and Chewbacca were yelling something he didn't want to take time to listen to, being in no mood for a debate. Losing patience, he threw off his flight jacket, stepped over the bow rail, sprang, and began drawing himself down the hawser, hand over hand, his legs wrapped around it, the higher swells wetting his back.

The shore-gang chief felt the vibrations in the hawser, saw Han, and sawed more furiously at the tough fiber. The chief took a moment to slash at the pilot. Han suddenly realized how impetuous he had been, as if another man entirely had occupied his body for a moment. He didn't quite avoid the stroke and the knifepoint cut across his chin. The water pulled at them both.

But Han avoided the back-slash with dexterity gained in zero-gee acrobatics drills. He lashed out flat-handed in a disarming blow, and the knife plunked into the water. As the knife fell, the shore-gang chief began to lose his grip on the hawser. He grabbed at Han, and both men plunged into the water. The lakewater was agonizingly cold and had a peculiar taste.

Han dove as deeply as he could, his clothes dragging at him. Underwater he heard the thud of the raft's bow striking the chief's head. Cheeks puffed, the pilot glanced up through the icy, dark water as the raft passed over him, and then surfaced just behind it. He grabbed for the stern rail, missed, and was himself grabbed.

Chewbacca pulled his partner over the stern rail in one motion just as the raft began drifting to a halt. Shaking wet hair out of his eyes, Han gave an involuntary cry of surprise, seeing why they had stopped. Kasarax's maneuver had been Shazeen's needed provocation for combat under Swimmer Law. Both the monstrous bulls had ducked out of their tow-harnesses; now they met in resolute battle.

They charged into collision, a butting of great heads whose report sounded like the crack of a tree trunk, and an impact of muscular necks and broad chests that sent waves racing outward. Neither seemed hurt as they circled for position, flippers

whipping the water into foam. The shore-gang boss
was paddling toward his raft, eager to be out of the
behemoths' way.

Han felt Bollux's hard finger tap his shoulder.
"You'll no doubt be wanting this, sir. I caught it before it could go overboard, but you didn't seem to
hear me call you." He passed over Han's blaster.

Without taking his eyes from the battle, Han promised, "I'm doubling your salary," ignoring the fact that
he had never paid the droid a thing.

Kasarax wailed; he had been too slow on the withdrawal after nipping Shazeen. The older bull hadn't
gotten a full grip with his fangs, and Kasarax had gotten away, but now blood flowed down his neck scales.
Kasarax, wild with rage, charged again.

Shazeen met him head-on, each of them trying to
butt and bite, to press the other under the surface,
shrieking and trumpeting. Shazeen failed to repel a
determined assault by Kasarax and slid back as the
younger creature surged up over him seeking a death
grip on his uncle's throat. But he had been too eager.
Shazeen had drawn him out and now the older bull
dropped his pretext and dove, rolling. His blunt tail
slammed Kasarax's skull, and the younger combatant
fell back in pain. They resumed butting heads, biting, thrashing flippers, and colliding with one another.

"Hang on!" warned Hasti, the only one who had
thought to watch for other danger. The raft shuddered
and timbers splintered as the bow was tipped into the
air.

It was one of Kasarax's followers, a very young bull
from the looks of him. He had closed crushing jaws on
the raft's stern, shaking it, spouting wrathful blasts
from his blowhole. He tore a meter-wide bite out of
the raft, spat the wood aside, then came at them again.
Han set his blaster to maximum power.

"Don't kill him!" Hasti shouted. "You'll have them
all down on us!"

As the sauropteroid butted the raft, nearly capsizing
it, Han bellowed. "What do you want me to do, sweetheart, bite him back?"

"Leave it to them," she answered, pointing. She

meant the other Swimmers, who were closing in. Kasarax's overeager follower had ignited a general fray. One—Han thought it was the female who had surfaced at the dock and offered support to Shazeen—kicked up an impressive bow-wave, making straight for the raft. But once again the creature closed jaws on the raft's stern.

The trick's to keep on breathing till help arrives, Han told himself. He spied the cone of gooey dough Hasti had brought, still more than half-full. He reached for it, calling, "Chewie! Lock hands!"

Han got to unsteady feet. The Wookiee reached out his long arm and caught Han's free hand, steadying him. The young bull had seen him coming and opened its maw, but when he pulled up short it closed its jaws with a crash and blew a geyser of spray through its blowhole.

When he saw the edges of the blowhole vibrate with the indrawing of breath, Han jammed the cone of dough down on it as hard as he could. It landed on the sucking blowhole with a peculiar *shloop!*

The Swimmer froze, its eyes bulging. Into what air passages and chambers the dough had been drawn, Han couldn't begin to guess. The creature shook, then exploded in a sneeze that convulsed him, kicking up a fountain of water and nearly blowing Han off the raft with the fish-scented gust.

At that moment Shazeen's friend arrived. She hit the younger creature and they battled furiously. All around, pairs of the creatures rolled, ducked, bit, and butted in pitched combat. Scaled hides took tremendous punishment and the sound threatened to deafen the humans; the turbulence promised to capsize the raft.

Han kept his attention riveted on Shazeen and Kasarax, thinking, *If that old bull loses, it'll be a wet stroll home. And the fish are biting today!*

Both bulls were torn and injured, chunks missing from each one's hide and flippers. The older one moved slowly, worn down by his nephew's youthful endurance. They rammed together for another fierce exchange. Surprisingly, Kasarax went under.

Shazeen sought to follow up his advantage but failed to keep track of his antagonist and circled aimlessly. The air was so full of pealing battle cries that Shazeen took no notice of his passengers' warnings. Kasarax had slyly and quietly surfaced behind his uncle and to his left, in the blind spot resulting from his missing eye. The younger Swimmer lunged with jaws gaping for a lethal grip at the base of his uncle's skull.

But Shazeen moved with abrupt speed, coming around and bringing his head up sharply, tagging Kasarax's chin with the boniest part of his foreskull. The crack echoed from the opposite lakeshore. Dazed by the terrible blow, Kasarax barely had time to wobble before Shazeen had his throat tightly between black jaws.

"That old con artist!" Badure whooped. Chewbacca and Hasti hugged, and Han leaned on the rail, laughing. Shazeen was shaking his nephew's head mercilessly, side to side and forward and back, but refraining from the death bite.

At last Kasarax, head bent back at a painful angle, no fight left in him, began a pitiful croaking. All around him, combat ceased at the sounds of ritualistic surrender. When all the others had separated, Kasarax was released and allowed to tread water meekly while his uncle stormed at him in the sibilant language of their kind.

With a final, piercing rebuke, Shazeen sent his nephew off with a hard butt of his head. Kasarax submitted, then stroked slowly away to haul his towraft back the way he had come. His followers trailed him in disarray, convoyed by Shazeen's victorious supporters.

Shazeen moved to his own raft, feeling the pain he hadn't allowed himself to show his enemies. Bleeding from fearsome wounds, his scarred, one-eyed head battered and torn, he asked, "Now then, where were we?"

"*I* was in the drink," Han reminded him. "*You* were hauling the raft around to take out the shore-gang boss. Got him right in the bulb, too. Thanks."

The old bull made a gurgling sound resembling a chuckle. "An accident, peewee; didn't I tell you it's un-Lawful to meddle in a human squabble?" He gurgled again, bringing his wide chest against the raft's stern and shoving toward the opposite shore.

"What about your nephew?" Hasti wanted to know.

"Oh, he's through trying to make the lake his own pond. Fool idea would have gotten him killed sooner or later anyway, and he's too valuable to waste. I'll need a deputy soon; haven't got many more scraps like that one left in me. These youngsters always think they're clever, going for my blind side."

"I still wouldn't trust him," Han warned.

"You don't trust *anybody*," Hasti chided.

"And you don't see me getting my flipper bit, do you?" he retorted smugly.

"Oh, Kasarax will be all right," Shazeen said. "He just thought he wanted us to fear him. He'll like it better once we respect him; all but the worst ones come around, given the chance."

The far shore had come up quickly. Shazeen propelled them toward it with a few more hard strokes, then flipped over and shoved them on with a sweep of his rear flippers. The raft nosed onto the strand, lifted on the crest. Han stepped onto the damp sand.

The others followed him. Badure had a rather sick Skynx slung over one shoulder. The female who had saved Shazeen's passengers surfaced next to him, obviously concerned.

But her eye fell on Hasti, whose cowl had fallen back to display her red hair. "You had a rougher ride this time, human," the Swimmer observed.

Hasti registered confusion. "Wasn't that you," the Swimmer female asked, "back before Kasarax took over? Sorry; the hair and, what do you call them, the clothes, are just the same."

Hasti whispered, "Lanni! These are her clothes!"

Badure asked the female what this passenger had done.

"Just came across and asked people questions about those mountains there, waved a little machine in the air, then went back," she replied.

Han, pouring water from his boot, looked up at the mountains rearing to the south. "What's up there?"

"Nothing," answered Shazeen. "Humans don't usually go up there. Fewer come back. They say it's just desolation up there." He was studying Chewbacca, who had doffed the hated cloak, Bollux's gleaming form, and the now-reviving Skynx.

"I'd heard that," agreed Badure. "The mining camp lies on the far side of the mountains, Han, but I'd reckoned we'd go around. Why should Lanni have been interested in them, I wonder?"

Han stood up. "Let's find out."

☐ X

THE terrain lifted away from the lakeshore in a series of rolling hills carpeted with soft, blue moss that cushioned their steps. Han was gratified to see the moss spring back when they had passed, thereby obliterating the group's prints.

Supplies were no problem. The workers on this side of the lake, all members of Kasarax's shore gang, had departed in haste on seeing their leader defeated, fearing the blood-vengeance of the non–gang members. Calculating a ten-to-twelve-day march through the mountains, the party had carefully picked through the abandoned storage buildings for provisions and equipment.

They had filled their packs with jars of lake crustaceans marinated in syrup, plastic cartons of the doughy stuff Hasti had first sampled, tubes of pickled vegetable slices, bags of meal, smoked fish, cured meat, and some hard purple sausages. Even though they carried capacious water bladders, they were relying on finding more water in the mountains. According to the survey map, there were abundant runoffs and fresh springwater throughout the area. Those who wore clothing had gathered cold weather gear. Han had pulled off his wet clothes, settling for a Dellaltian outfit until he could dry his own, and contrived a bandage for the knife cut. Practicality had made Hasti exchange her robes and gown for an outfit suitable for an adolescent boy. They had also found thick, insulated bedrolls.

There were no riding animals or power vehicles to be found. But Han didn't mind, trusting unfamiliar beasts no more than he did the aged and breakdown-

prone Dellaltian machinery. Bollux, who could bear
a heavy pack and yet consumed no water or food,
found that his popularity had increased. They felt lucky
to have him along, knowing none of the local do-
mesticated animals or ground vehicles were suited to
the mountain terrain and aircraft were few and far
between on Dellalt. They had found some lengths of
rope, but no other climbing gear. Neither had they
found medicine or a medi-pack, additional weapons
or charges, commo or navigational gear, heating unit,
or macrobinoculars or tele-eye, though the scope on
Han's blaster would be some compensation for the
last. For shelter, they had brought along a wagoner's
tent they found in one of the abandoned buildings.

And they were armed. In addition to Han's side
arm and Chewbacca's bowcaster, they also had the
weapons captured from J'uoch's forces. Badure carried the stun-gun he had already used and a brace
of long-barreled power pistols. Hasti had a compact
disruptor, a dart-shooter loaded with toxic missiles,
and a blaster, but the latter was nearly exhausted
because Han had used it to recharge his own. Skynx
declined to bear arms, which his species never used,
and Bollux's basic programming, the droid said,
prohibited him from using them as well.

Ascending the foothills, they kept the ridge lines
between themselves and the region behind, though
Han doubted anyone was taking time to try to spot
them. The collapse of Kasarax's racket was probably
occupying everyone's attention. Gusting winds tore
across the open hills, pressing at the resilient moss
and stirring the travelers' hair, clothing, and fur. The
country was stark and vacant. Lacking a second
comlink, they decided not to put out a point-walker,
but rather to rely on the wide field of surveillance
they could maintain.

Chewbacca took the lead, treading the blue moss
lightly for all his size, testing the air with black nostrils
flaring. His blue eyes moved constantly, his hunter's
senses keenly attuned. A dozen paces behind trudged
Bollux. The labor droid had opened his chest plastron

a crack at the computer's demand, and Max was taking in the view.

Next came Badure and Hasti side by side. Skynx followed after, carrying only his musical instruments because none of the packs fit him and he couldn't have borne much weight anyway. Undulating along, he kept pace without difficulty.

Han brought up the rear, frequently casting glances behind, making minute adjustments in the balance and shoulder-strap padding of the makeshift pack he had thrown together. He lined up prominent terrain features and did his best to keep track of their direction and course, since that was the only way they would have of orienting themselves to the surveying map. From time to time he thought about the treasure, but the open countryside and the brisk wind made him happier than he would have admitted. In a way, they reminded him of the freedom of space travel.

The group moved on throughout the morning with deliberate speed, Han stopping frequently to scan his blaster's scope for some sign of pursuit. But as Dellalt's blue-white primary climbed the sky and none appeared, they slowed a bit, saving strength for the long journey.

Skynx dropped back to talk to Han. The Ruurian had a rapid metabolism and so had recovered from his bout with the flask. Han, who had been walking backward for a few paces while he checked the rear, pivoted around in step. It occurred to him that Skynx must be thoroughly disillusioned with human-style adventuring.

"Hey, Skynx, break out that hip-pocket orchestra of yours. We're out in the open anyway, like a bug on a canopy. A little music won't make things any chancier."

The Ruurian complied eagerly. Using his lowermost four sets of limbs for locomotion without decreasing speed, he took up the tympanic pulsers, bellows-horn, and flute. He began a human-tempo marching tune, one for marching overland rather than for a parade. The small pulsers held a catchy beat, the bellows-horn tootled, and the flute skirled. Han resisted the quickened pace, but enjoyed the music.

Badure squared his shoulders and fell into energetic stride, sucking in his overhanging stomach and humming with the music. Hasti smiled at Skynx and strode along more quickly.

Chewbacca tried to stay in step, although Wookiees don't generally take to regimentation. The process was awkward for him. He achieved a kind of animated swagger, though not even remotely in time. Bollux, however, fell right into step, mechanical legs pumping precisely, arms swinging, chin held high.

They trod blue moss; cold wind made the landscape seem barren and free. In this manner they proceeded over the hill.

They were well up into the heights when the bluewhite sun set. The few lights of the city came on, far below and behind them. Outcroppings of rock had begun to appear, rising from the blue moss. They camped at one of these ledges, under an overhang that would afford some protection from wind. There was no fuel for a fire.

As they settled in, Han established priorities. "I'm going to check the area with the scope. Chewie will take first watch, after he eats. Badure, you take second and I'll take third. Skynx can have the wake-up duty. Is that all right with everybody?"

Badure didn't mention Han's assumption of leadership, being content with the arrangement. "What about me?" Hasti asked evenly.

"You can have first watch tomorrow, so don't feel left out. Would it be straining our bonds of affection to ask to borrow your wrist chrono?"

Teeth clenched, she threw it at him, then he and Chewbacca set off. "You're welcome!" she called after him. "Who does he think he is, anyway?" she said to the others.

Badure answered mildly. "Slick? He's used to taking charge; he wasn't always a smuggler and a freighter bum. Didn't you notice the red piping on the

seams of his shipboard trousers? They don't give away
the Corellian Bloodstripe for perfect attendance."

She considered that for a moment. "Well, how did
he get it? And why do you call him Slick?"

"You'll have to get that first part from him, but
the nickname business goes back to the first time I
met him, way back."

In spite of herself, she was curious. Skynx was
also listening with interest, as were Bollux and Blue
Max. The two automata decided to hear Badure out
before shutting down for the night; their photoreceptors glowed in the dusk.

It was becoming colder fast, and the humans pulled
their cloaks tighter, Badure closing his flight jacket.
Skynx curled his woolly form to conserve body heat.

"I'd been a line officer, had a few decorations myself," Badure began, "but there was the matter of a
floating Jubilee Wheel I was running onboard the
flagship. Anyway, they reassigned me to the staff at
an academy.

"The commandant was a desk pilot, off his gyros.
His bright idea was to take a training ship, an old
U-33 orbital loadlifter, and rig her so the flight instructor could cause malfunctions: *realistic stress situations.*

" 'Enough can go wrong without building more into
a ship,' I said, but the commandant had pull. His
program was approved. I was flight instructor, and
the commandant came along on the first training
mission. He gave the briefing himself, playing up the
wise old veteran act.

"In the middle of it a cadet interrupted. 'Excuse
me, sir, but the U-33's primary thrust sequence is
four-stage, not three.' The kid was gangly, all elbows
and ears, and had this big chow-eating grin.

"The commandant was cold as permafrost. 'Since
Cadet Solo is such a slick student, he will be first in
the hotseat.' We all boarded and took off. Han handled
everything the C.O. threw at him, and that grin grew
bigger and bigger. He really had put in a lot of time
on that kind of ship.

"That crate had checked out one hundred percent, but something went wrong and something blew; a second later we had all we could do to keep her in the air. I couldn't get the landing gear to extend, so I raised ground control and asked for emergency tractor retrieval.

"And the tractors failed, primaries and secondaries both, on the approach run. I just managed to get us up again. The commandant was white around the eyes by then; the crash wagons and firefighting machinery were deploying onto the field.

"Which was when Cadet Solo announced, 'The reservoir-locking valve on the landing gear's stuck shut, sir; these U-33's do it all the time.'

"And I said, 'Well, do you feel like crawling down into the gear bay and taking a wrench to it right this second?'

"'No need,' the kid says, 'We can joggle it with a couple of maneuvers.'

"The commandant's teeth were rattling. 'You can't take a bulk vessel through aerobatics!' Then I said, 'You hope to sit in your mess kit I can't, sir, because I don't know which maneuvers Slick over there is talking about. He'll have to do it.' While his mouth was hanging open, I reminded him he was ranking officer. 'Either you land this beast or let the kid try out his idea.'

"He shut up, but about that time there was a rumpus in the passenger compartment. The other cadets were becoming nervous. So Han opened the intercom. 'By order of the commandant, this is a full-dress emergency-landing *drill*. All procedures will be observed; you are being graded on your performance.'

"I told him he was playing fast and loose with what might be somebody's last moments, and he told me to go ahead and tell them the truth if I wanted a panic in the hold. I let it ride. Han took control back.

"The U-33 isn't designed for the things Han did to that bird. He took her through three inverted outside loops to free up the locking claws. Our vision began to go. How Han coaxed lift from those inverted wings, I'll never know; but he was smirking, hanging there from his harness.

"He went into barrel rolls to build centrifugal force in the reservoir. I thought he was going to rip the wings off and I almost took control back, but just then I got a board light. He had forced the valve open.

"But gravity could've swung it shut again, so he had to fly upside-down while the landing gear cranked out. The ship had begun losing altitude and the commandant was sort of frothing at the mouth, babbling for Han to pull out. Han refused. 'Wait for it, wait for it,' he said. Then we heard this long grinding sound as the landing gear seated, and a clang as it locked.

"Han snap-rolled, hit full reverse thrusters, and hung out all the hardware. We uprooted two stopnets and only lived because we landed into the wind. Jouncer landing, I tell you.

"They had to help the commandant off the ship. Then they deactivated that ship for good. Han locked down his board, just like the rule book says. 'Slick enough for you?' he asked. I said 'Slick.' That's how the nickname started."

It was fully dark now. The stars were luminous overhead, and both of Dellalt's moons were in the sky. "Badure, if it happened today," Hasti asked quietly, "would you tell those cadets they might die?"

He sounded tired. "Yes. Even though they might've panicked. They had a right to know."

The logical next question, then, was, "Well, what're *our* chances, the truth? Can we get the *Falcon* back, or even survive an attempt?" Skynx, and the automata, too, hung on his reply.

Badure remained silent. Through his mind passed the options: lying, telling the truth, or simply rolling over and going to sleep. But when he opened his mouth to answer, he was interrupted.

"Depends on what we run up against," Han Solo said from the darkness, having returned so quietly that they hadn't heard him. "If camp security's loose, we could get away without losses. If it's tight, we

have to tackle them somehow, maybe draw them
out. Anyway, it means risk. We'd probably have
casualties and some of us might not make it."

"*Some?* Admit it, Solo; you're so concerned with getting that ship of yours back that you're ignoring facts.
J'uoch's got more hired killers than—"

"J'uoch's got portside brawlers and some small-
time muscle," Han corrected Hasti. "If they were
quality, they wouldn't be working for a two-credit
outfit like hers. Handing some clod a gun doesn't
make him a gunman."

He stepped closer and she could see his silhouette
against the stars. "They have the numbers, but the
only real gunman within light-years is standing right
in front of you."

The craft was trim, sleek, luxuriously customized,
a scoutship off the military inventory. Her approach
and landing were exacting, and she set down precisely where the *Millennium Falcon* had landed several
days earlier. Her lone occupant emerged.

The man was limber, graceful, though his movements were at times abrupt. Although he was tall and
lean, his form seemed compact. His clothes were expensive and impeccable, of the finest materials, but
somber—gray trousers and a high-collared white shirt
with a short gray jacket over it. A long white scarf,
knotted at his throat, fell in soft folds, and his black
shoes shone. He wore his graying hair cropped short,
but his mustachios were long, their ends gathered and
weighted with two tiny golden beads, giving him a sub-
tly roguish look.

Townspeople appeared and clustered around him,
just as they had greeted the *Falcon*'s passengers. But
something in this stranger's blue, unblinking eyes,
something penetrating and without mercy, made them
wary. He soon obtained from them the story of the
Falcon's arrival and removal by the mining-camp ship.
They showed him the spot where the spaceboat had
been destroyed by the lighter. Even scavengers had
avoided the bits of wreckage, fearing radiation resi-
dues.

The stranger told the townspeople to disperse, and seeing the look in his eyes, they obeyed. He carefully removed his jacket and hung it inside his ship. Around his waist an intricately tooled black gunbelt held a blaster high on his right hip.

He brought certain sensitive instruments from his ship, some on a carrying harness, others attached to a long probe, and still others set in a very sophisticated remote-globe. Loosening his scarf, he made a patient examination of the area, working in a careful pattern.

An hour later he returned the equipment to his ship and rubbed the dust from his gleaming shoes with a rag. He was satisfied that no one had died when J'uoch's spaceboat had been destroyed. He reknotted his scarf while he considered the situation.

Eventually, Gallandro drew on his jacket and locked up his ship, then made his way into the city. He soon heard rumors of bizarre goings-on down at the lake and battles among the natives. He couldn't verify much about the outside humans involved, though; the only close-range witnesses, the shore gang of the sauropteroid Kasarax, had gone into hiding. Still, he was willing to credit the story. It was in keeping with Han Solo's wildly unpredictable luck.

No, Gallandro corrected himself. "Luck" was what Solo would have called it. He, Gallandro, had long ago rejected mysticism and superstition. It made it that much more frustrating to see how events seemed to conspire to impel Solo along.

Gallandro intended to prove that Solo was no more than he appeared to be, a small-time smuggler of no great consequence. That the gunman had doubtless given the matter far more thought than Solo himself was a source of ironic amusement to him. Using the vast resources of his employer, the Corporate Sector Authority, he had tracked Solo and the Wookiee this far and would, with only a little more patience, complete the hunt.

☐ XI

"THERE'S something wrong," Han said, peering intently through his blaster's scope in the morning light. "I'm not sure, but— Here, you look, Badure."

"It just looks like a landing field to me," Hasti commented.

"Just because it's big and flat and has ships parked on it?" Han asked sarcastically. "Don't jump to any conclusions; after all, we may've stumbled onto the only used-aircraft lot in these mountains."

A stiff breeze at their backs blew down the narrow valley toward the field. It had been snowing heavily in the region; at the far edge of the flat area below, a snowfield sloped sharply downward toward the lowlands.

"It's not on any map I ever saw," declared Badure, squinting through the scope.

"Doesn't mean a thing," Han replied. "The Tion. Hegemony's survey-updating program is running something like a hundred and eighty years behind schedule and getting worse. And these mountains are full of turbulence and storm activity. A survey-flyover ship could've missed that place altogether. Even an Alpha Team or a full Beta Mission might not have caught it."

Thinking it over, Han rubbed his jaw, feeling his growth of beard. He, like the others, was drawn and haggard from the march and had lost a good deal of weight. The knife cut across his chin was healing well enough in the absence of a medi-pack.

"Badure's right," Hasti said, holding the survey-map reader up close to her face. "There's nothing on here at all. And what's it doing out here anyway? Look, they had to have carved away half that cliff to build it."

Han was concentrating on the field with his remarkably acute vision. There, guidance lights and warning beacons were dark, understandable at a hidden base; but they seemed to be of a very outdated design. He could make out several craft that appeared to be about the size of spaceboats, and five larger ones. It was difficult to see any details because their tails and afterburners were pointed in his direction. Then he knew what was bothering him.

"Badure, they've got those ships parked and tied down with their rear ends into the wind." Since the craft on the field followed common aerodynamic design principles, the sensible way to position them would have been with their noses into the prevailing air currents.

Badure lowered the scope and handed back Han's blaster. "The wind's been steady, at least since last night. Either they don't care what kind of knocking-around their ships will take if a storm kicks up, or the place is deserted."

"We haven't seen a soul down there," Hasti said.

Han turned to Bollux. "Are you still getting those signals?"

"Yes, Captain. They originate from that antenna mast down there by the field, I would say. They're very weak. I only picked them up because the summit we climbed was close on a direct line of sight."

Han and Bollux had ascended that summit, a laborious session of trudging and scrambling and occasionally climbing, because of a suspicion of Han's. In the mining camp, Hasti and Badure had heard rumors that J'uoch and her partners were increasing camp security. Adding to that an apparent interest in the mountains on the part of Lanni, Hasti's late sister, Han thought it possible the mountains were seeded with antipersonnel sensors that were somehow tied in with the treasure. On the chance that, if there were sensors, they would be active rather than passive and therefore detectable, Han had taken the futilely protesting labor droid up to see if, now that they were approaching the lowlands,

they could detect any signals. Using his built-in
command-signal receiver, Bollux had tried all the
standard calibrations and, when those yielded nothing,
sampled others. Finally he had picked up a signal of a
long-outmoded sort, and Han had taken a rough fix on
it. The signal had led the group to this narrow valley,
and the morning revealed what was apparently a landing field bracketed in stone.

They had been marching through the mountains for
days; songs and high spirits had given way to sore
feet, overworked servo-motors, aching muscles, and
shoulders chafed by pack straps. The visit to the spa at
the University of Rudrig seemed to Han like a dream
of another life. According to the map, they were very
nearly through the mountains.

That map had turned out to be their most important
piece of equipment, allowing them to choose the
easiest course. Nonetheless, they had hit a number of
places where they had had to climb, where Skynx suddenly became a major asset. The Ruurian could scale
or descend sheer rock faces, carrying one end of a
climbing rope with him. Without Skynx, Han knew,
they would still be somewhere far back in the mountains. As it was, their food was running low. Fortunately they had managed to find water on their route.

But even after they left the mountains they would
still have to cross an expanse of open plains before
reaching the mining site. A common thought was running through the group's respective biological and
synthetic synapses: acquisition of a ship, even an at-
mospheric craft, would mark an end to their walking
days. In addition, the field might offer supplies as well
as transportation.

"Could this be what Lanni was curious about?"
Badure wondered aloud.

"We'll see," Han decided. They had concealed
themselves behind some rocks within a kilometer of
the field. "Chewie and I'll go in first. If we give the all-
clear sign, come on down." He demonstrated a broad
waving motion, left to right. "But if we don't signal
you within a half hour, or we give you *any* other kind
of signal, get yourselves out of here. Write us off and

try to reach the mining site, or double back to the city if that's what seems best."

Han and the Wookiee started shedding their extra gear. "I'm not so sure we shouldn't have stayed in the city," said Hasti.

Han tried to reassure her. "You would be if you'd ever done any time swabbing out the plumbing in some local lockup, doll. You ready, Chewie?"

He was. They moved out, taking turns advancing from cover to cover. Each awaited the other's hand motion before moving; they had done this sort of thing together before.

They observed no sentries, patrols, watchtowers, or surveillance equipment as they approached; but they felt no less uneasy. When at last they reached the edge of the field, they held a brief but heated debate conducted entirely in hand signals, over who would be first to step into the open. Each insisted that he should be the one. Han cut the dispute short, just before it devolved into an exchange of angry gestures, by rising and stepping out from the cover of the boulder.

Chewbacca, eyes roving the scene, bowcaster raised and ready, immediately shifted to a position from which he could give supporting fire. Han slowly moved across the open area, blaster out, nerves taut.

No shot or outcry came—and no alarm. The field was a simple expanse of flat ground—partly smoothed soil and partly rock that, from the looks of it, had been leveled a long time ago. Han wondered why somebody hadn't done a complete job and paved it over with formex or some other surfacing material.

He saw no buildings of any kind—only the primitive antenna mast, ground beacons, ground-control light clusters, and area illumination banks. He skirted the edge of the field, darting in among the rocks without warning to make sure no one was waiting in ambush.

He reemerged and continued working his way toward the parked ships. When he was satisfied that nobody had a gun turret or missile tube pointed at him from one of the craft, he approached them. And when

he had come close enough to make out detail, he had
difficulty speaking for a second.

What the flaming— "Hey, Chewie! Get over here!"

The Wookiee was out in the open instantly, racing
toward him, bowcaster held high. His charge slowed to
a distracted lope, then immobility as he saw what Han
was talking about. He gave a bemused, lowing sound.

"That's right," Han agreed, slamming the side of one
of the ships with his fist. It gave, leaving a deep inden-
tation. "They're phonies."

Chewbacca came up slowly, shouldering his
weapon, and took a firm grasp on the hatch of the next
ship in line. He tore it off easily: it was merely a
mockup constructed of treated extrusion sheeting and
light structural alloys. He cast the hatch aside with a
brayed Wookiee imprecation and leaned into the open
hatchway. Light came through the clear pane used to
simulate the cockpit windshield. The dummy ship,
ribbed by support members, was gloomy, stale-
smelling, and empty.

Han, examining the ships and the general layout of
the field, was stumped. Nonetheless, he kept his pistol
in his hand. The mockups were crude but had been
made with obvious attention to details of landing gear,
fuselage, propulsors, and control surfaces. They were
copied—at least, he presumed them to have been
copied—from models he didn't recognize and secured
in place with lines of some artificial fiber.

His first thought was that this was a decoy base,
part of some military campaign or defense system. But
there had been no organized conflict on Dellalt or, for
that matter, in this sector of space for years and years.
Furthermore, this fake landing field must demand a
certain amount of upkeep to be in the shape it was. A
trick of J'uoch's? No logic sustained that.

Chewbacca was more instinctive. In his mind the
place conjured images of some malign force using the
field as a sort of trap, like those of the webweavers on
the lower tree levels of his home planet. Nervously
glancing around, eager to be away, he set one paw
against Han's shoulder to get him moving.

The pilot shrugged off the paw. "Take it easy, will

you? This place might still have some stuff we can use. Take a quick look around while I check out that antenna mast."

The Wookiee shambled off unenthusiastically. He made a rapid, thorough sweep of the area, discovering no watchers, no tracks, nor any fresh scents.

When Chewbacca returned, Han straightened from his examination of the instrument pods at the mast. "It runs off some kind of sealed power plant, a little one. It might have started broadcasting yesterday or been going for years and years. I gave the others the signal to come ahead."

Chewbacca whined unhappily, wanting only to depart from this place. Han was losing patience. "Chewie, I'm getting tired of this. There's receiver gear here that we can use to check for sensors and get a bearing on J'uoch's mining camp. This thing's been beaming for a whole day at least; if anybody in this miserable solar system were coming, they'd be here by now." That made the entire installation much more of a curiosity, he had to admit; but he didn't mention it, not wanting to make his towering sidekick any more nervous than he already was.

Badure, Hasti, Skynx, and Bollux soon appeared and, when they had looked over the bogus landing field, voiced surprise and mystification.

"This isn't any part of J'uoch's operation, I'm sure," Hasti said. Badure didn't add anything, but his expression conveyed discomfort. Skynx's antennae were waving a little erratically, but Han chalked that up to the Ruurian's timidity.

"All right," the pilot said briskly. "If we work fast, we'll be out of here inside of an hour. Bollux, I want to patch you and Max in on some of the equipment; one of Max's adaptor arms ought to fit. The rest of you fan out and keep your eyes open. Hey, Skynx, you feeling okay?"

The little Ruurian's antennae were waving even more pronouncedly now. His head wobbled for a moment, then he shook himself. "Yes, I—felt strange for a second, Captain. Strain of the journey, I should imagine."

"Well, hang in there, old fellow. You'll make it." Han started off with the labor droid while the others began spreading out.

Then he heard a panicked squeak and whirled to see Skynx collapse in a multilegged heap, antennae vibrating. "Stay away from him!" Han shouted.

Hasti fairly jumped back. "What's happened to him?"

"I don't know, but it's not going to happen to us." They had too few facts to decide with any accuracy what was wrong with him; it could be a disease, or something natural to his peculiar physiology, perhaps even a part of the Ruurian life cycle. But Han wasn't going to risk having any other living members of the party contaminated. "Bollux, pick him up; we're pulling out of here. Everybody else, cover."

They formed a ring, weapons ready, as the labor droid hoisted the small, limp form and held it easily in his gleaming arms. Han barked out instructions. "Chewie, take the lead." But as they moved out Han found his own vision becoming blurry.

He shook his head violently, which helped, but a surge of alarm made his breathing more rapid, and his heart began pumping furiously. They had only gone a few more paces when Badure, opening his flight jacket's collar, slurred: "Whatever it is, I'm in it with Skynx." He collapsed to the ground without another word, but his eyes remained open, his breathing regular.

Hasti rushed to him, but she, too, was already unsteady on her feet. Chewbacca would have put out a paw to support her, but Han snagged a handful of his partner's pelt and pulled him back. "No, Chewie. We've got to get clear before it happens to us." Han knew that they might be able to come back and help the others later, but if they succumbed now, no one was likely to survive.

Without warning, Han's legs gave way. The Wookiee, chugging like a steam engine, shifted his bowcaster to one hand and reached for his friend. His prodigious strength seemed to give him additional resistance to whatever was affecting the others. He

considered running for it, for Han's statement that
someone must get clear was correct. But the Wookiee
code of ethics left no room for desertion. Tugging at
his friend, he made a mournful sound.

Chewbacca wrestled his partner's slack body up
onto his shoulder. Han, eyes still open, unable to
speak, watched dully as the world spun by. Showing
his fangs, the Wookiee put one broad foot in front of
the other with determination. After a gallant struggle
that brought him almost to the edge of the field,
Chewbacca sank to his knees, nearly struggled up
again, then pitched forward. Han regretted numbly
that he couldn't tell his friend what a good try it had
been.

Bollux now found himself in a crisis of decision—
all actions and inactions pointed to members of the
group coming to harm or dying. Resolving a course
of action nearly burned out his basic logic stacks.
Then the droid put Skynx down, and the Ruurian
curled up into a ball by reflex. Bollux began the task
of dragging Han Solo to safety. The pilot was, in the
droid's evaluation, the one most likely to aid the
others by virtue of his talents, turn of mind, and stub-
bornness.

As it happened, Chewbacca's fall had left Han in
a position from which he could see Bollux approach.
He wanted to tell the droid to take Chewbacca instead, but could form no words. Han's view of the
droid was suddenly blocked by fantastic figures that
leaped, capered, and circled around Bollux, gesturing
and gibbering at him. They were dressed in bright
costumes that were half-uniform, half-masquerade
costume, and wore fantastic headgear, elaborate con-
trivances that suggested both helmet and mask. Even
in his stupor Han registered the fact that they carried
firearms of diverse types. Han thought them to be
humans.

After a quick conference among themselves, the
new arrivals began to push, pull, and shoo the dis-
traught droid, forcing him out of Han's field of vision.
The pilot was unable to move his head to follow the
action.

A masked head thrust in close to him, examining him, but Han couldn't move back or even flinch. The globular mask bore a strong resemblance to a high-altitude or spacesuit helmet, but many of the details of instrumentation, pressure valves, hookups, and couplings were painted on. The air hoses and power-supply cords were useless tubes that dangled and swirled as the mask moved. Unintelligible words in a male human voice rang hollowly.

Han felt himself being lifted, but distantly, as if he had been packed in a crate of dunnage beads. Incidental views showed him that the same was happening to all the others except Bollux, who seemed to have disappeared altogether.

Then came a ride of uncertain duration. The lay of the land and the vagaries of the portage showed Han the rocky ground, Dellalt's blue-white sun, his companions being carried along by other captors, and then the ground again, with no predictability.

At last he saw a gaping hole in the terrain, an entrance to a subsurface area three times the size of the *Falcon*'s main hatch. The boulder that had hidden it was raised on six thick support jacks. Lowered, it would seal and camouflage the hole perfectly, Han knew, because he himself had prowled past it earlier in investigating the area.

Wide pleated hoses had been brought up from beneath the surface. Their pulsations indicated that a gas was being pumped through them, but Han could detect nothing by sight or smell. This was how they had been paralyzed, then; he concluded dizzily that the fantastic headgear he had seen contained breathing filters or respirators.

His bearers moved toward the opening. Suddenly darkness swirled all around him. Either he drifted into and out of consciousness or the lighting in the underground area was only intermittent; it was impossible to tell which. He knew that once or twice he caught sight of the sources of illumination: primitive glow-rods arcing over the tunnels, like tracer trails of rockets, in soft colors of blue and green and red.

Han was carried past many rooms that seemed to

serve a wide variety of functions. Once he heard sounds of adults chanting, then of children doing the same. There were the rhythms of heavy machinery, whirring turbines and banging switching panels, racing gears and the spitting, crackling openings and closings of massive power bars. He smelled foods that were strange to him, and people, with all their various odors.

He tried to concentrate, either to find a way out of his predicament or to experience his last moments fully, but instead kept drifting into passivity.

His first indication that the paralysis was wearing off was when he was unceremoniously dumped onto a cold stone floor; he didn't quite let out a yelp but came close. He hurt where he had hit: his shoulder, back, and rump.

He heard someone—Badure, he thought—groan. Han tried to sit up. A bad mistake; a flare ignited in his forehead. He lay back down, knowing now what had elicited Badure's groan. He clasped his forehead, a major victory of movement, and ran his tongue over his teeth, checking to see if fungus were really growing there.

Suddenly an enormous shaggy face was hovering over him. Chewbacca hauled him up by great fistsful of his flight jacket and sat him up against a large stone. Han's faltering hand went automatically to his holster and found it vacant. That frightened him, but galvanized him as well.

He clamped both hands to his head, whispering so that it wouldn't come apart. "Best time to escape's the soonest," he told his first mate. "Kick the door over and let's leg it."

His friend urrffed with a disgusted gesture to the door. Han made a major effort and looked up, setting off little shooting stars on the periphery of his vision.

The door was barely discernible, an oblong of stone fitted into the wall so tightly that barely a hairline crack showed. There was a glow-rod on either side of it, but the rest of the room was unlit. Han frisked himself—no tools, no weapons, not even a toothpick.

Badure and Hasti had been dumped together. Skynx was still rolled in a tight ball, but of Bollux there was no sign. The Wookiee plucked Han to his feet, and the pilot moved to one of the glow-rods and pulled it from its socket. The filament retained enough power to run independently for some time. Han moved farther into the chamber, waving the light as he explored; his partner trailed behind, huge fists ready.

"Check the size of this place!" Han found the breath to whisper. The Wookiee grunted. The stone ceiling arced away into the gloom beyond the light. Han came upon row after long row of low stone monoliths, about the height of his sternum, twice as wide as they were high. He couldn't see an end to them.

A voice behind them made both partners jump. "Where *are* we?" It was Hasti, who had just recovered enough to rise and follow. "And what are those things? Shelves? Work tables?"

"Runways?" Han added, wincing at the throbbing in his head. "Paperweights? Who knows? Let's look the rest of this granite gymnasium over." *At least,* he thought, *moving about would help counteract the paralysis. Best to let the others rest for now.*

But a search of the gargantuan room, which was about the size and shape of a medium spacecraft hangar, yielded no other doors, no other features at all, simply a vast space filled with the stone slabs.

"The whole mountain's probably hollow," Han conjectured, keeping his voice low. "But I don't see how those hopping half-wits we saw could've done it." They started back toward the door.

Chewbacca uttered a low sound.

Han translated. "He's saying how dry it is in here. You'd expect it to be damp, from condensation if nothing else." Their footsteps clacked and echoed.

By that time Badure was sitting up and Skynx had uncurled. Interrupting one another with several simultaneous conversations and frequent crossovers, they established the bare facts of what had happened.

"What will they do with us?" Skynx asked, not concealing his trembling.

"Who knows?" Han responded. "But they took

Bollux and Max. I hope those two lads don't end up as drill bits and belt buckles." He regretted now his own and Chewbacca's abuse of the aircraft mockups on the landing field, and wondered if this was the standard treatment of vandals, recalling the Swimmer Shazeen's comment that few travelers made it through the mountains. "Anyway, they haven't killed us out of hand; that's one thing in our favor, right?" Skynx did not seem comforted.

"I'm thirsty," Hasti announced, "and hungry as a Wookiee."

"I'll summon room service," offered Han. "Marinated range-squab for four, and a few magnums of chilled *T'iil-T'iil?* We'll get the place redecorated while we're at it."

She snorted. "You should get the auto-valet, Solo, and feed yourself into it; you look like a jet-juicer just off an eight-day twister."

Amused, Han glanced at her, giving her a long-suffering smile. Then he sighed and sat down with his back against one of the stone slabs. Chewbacca lowered himself next to Han. "Hey, partner; forward guard to your center's flanking slot, six win-lose units."

Chewbacca fell into deep concentration, chin on fist, envisioning the gameboard match they would be playing on the *Falcon*. Without computer assistance, playing was much more difficult and involved, but it might help pass the time.

Hasti went to stand before the chamber's single door. Han looked up and saw that her shoulders were shaking, as was the glow-rod she held in her hand. He got up and went to comfort her, assuming she was weeping, but she pushed his hand away, and it dawned on him that she was trembling in anger.

Without warning, the girl flung herself at the door, swinging the glow-rod. It burst into splinters and a shower of sparks and blazing shards. She pounded the stone with the stump of the glow-rod, kicking it and beating it with her free hand, ranting maledictions she had learned in a life among the mining camps and factory worlds of the Tion Hegemony.

Han and Badure approached her when the worst

of her rage seemed spent. "Nobody's locking me under some old mountain to rot!" she yelled. She swung randomly at the men with the battered stump of the glow-rod, and they found it more politic to duck than to grapple. "Part of that treasure's mine, and nobody better try to cut me out of it!"

Puffing, drained, she shuffled over to where the Wookiee sat. Chewbacca had watched the proceedings curiously. Hasti dropped the glow-rod stump and sat down next to the *Millennium Falcon*'s first mate.

Han was about to say something, if only to comment on the intensity of her avarice, when a glissando from Skynx's flute sounded through the room.

The Ruurian still wore his instruments. They had been cradled to his middle, concealed by his woolly coat, when he had curled up. He was tuning them in an absorbed way, shutting out his current distress, having perched on the slab against which Chewbacca and Hasti sat.

Han went to listen while Badure stayed at the door to study it with the remaining glow-rod. In the half-light Skynx played a haunting tune full of longing and loneliness. Han dropped down next to Hasti and together they listened. The music made strange play with the acoustics of the vast space.

Skynx paused. "This is a song of my home colony, you see. It's called 'By the Banks of the Warm, Pink Z'gag.' It's played at cocoon-weaving time, when the cycle's crop of larvae gather to go chrysalis. At the same time the previous cycle's cocoons open and the chroma-wings come forth to exude their pheromones, which draw them to one another. The air is sweet and light then; gaiety is there."

A large globule of emotion-secretion gathered at the corner of each faceted red eye. "This adventuring has been educational, but most of it is nothing more than danger and hardship a very long way from home. If I were ever to come to the banks of the Z'gag again, I would never leave!" He resumed playing the sad melody.

Hasti, gazing vacantly into the darkness, was di-

sheveled, but looked attractive nonetheless, nearly
as pretty as when she had been gowned and primped
onboard the *Falcon*. Han slipped an arm around her
and she leaned against him, scarcely noticing him.

"Don't fold until the hand's over," he encouraged
her quietly.

She turned to him with a labored smile, brushing
her dirty fingers against his stubble of beard, tracing
the raw scar across his chin. "You know, this is an
improvement, Solo. You're not Slick now, not so
smooth and careless."

He leaned toward her and she didn't turn away.
And then he kissed her. There was some question as
to who was more surprised. Without parting, they
settled into a more comfortable embrace, and gave
the kiss serious attention. Skynx's music carried them
along.

She shoved herself free at last. "Han, oh, I—stop
it; please, stop!" He retreated, confused. "The last
thing I need is to get involved with you."

Sounding wounded, he asked, "What's wrong with
me?"

"You run all over people and you never take anything seriously, for starters. You joke through life
with that silly smirk on your face, so sure of yourself
I want to bounce a rock off your skull!"

She kept him at arm's length. "Solo, my sister
Lanni inherited Dad's Guild book, so she had pilot's
status here in the Tion. But I had to work any job I
could get. Mess-hand, housegirl, sanit-crew, I've done
them all in the camps, the mines, the factories. I've
seen your type all my life. Everything's a big laugh,
and you can charm the daylights out of people when
you feel like it, but you're gone the next day and you
never look back. Han, there are no *people* in your
life!"

He protested, "Chewie—"

"—is your friend," she cut him off, "but he's a
Wookiee. And you've got that pair of mechanical
cohorts, Max and Bollux, and that hotshot starship
of yours, but the rest of us are temporary cargo. Where
are the people, Han?"

He started to defend himself, but she overrode him. Chewbacca, intrigued, forgot about his next game-board move.

"I'm sure you drive the portside girls wild, Solo; you look like you just stepped out of a holo-thriller. But I'm not one of them; never was, never will be."

She softened a bit. "I'm no different from Skynx. On my birthworld there's a stretch of land my parents used to own. I'm going to get my cut of the treasure, I swear on my blisters, and buy it back if I have to purchase the whole planet. I'll build a home and take care of Badure, because he took care of Lanni and me. I'll have things of my own and a *life* of my own. I'll share it if I meet the right man, but I'll live without him if I don't. Solo, light housekeeping in a starship isn't my idea of a dream come true!" She drew away from him and went to join Badure, pushing her fingers through the tangles of red hair.

Skynx finished his sad song, then lowered his flute. "I wish I could see the home colony one more time, the air filled with the chroma-wings and their phero-mones and the sounds of their wooing. What would you wish for, Captain Solo?"

Staring absently after Hasti, Han shrugged. "Stronger pheromones."

Skynx started. Then, sides rippling, began chortling in the Ruurian version of convulsive laughter, issuing chittering, high-pitched giggles. Chewbacca loosed a sustained howl of amusement, slapping his thigh with a huge paw, his mane shaking. That started Han chuck-ling ruefully. He reached up and gave Skynx a push; the Ruurian rolled over onto his back, tittering and kicking his short limbs in the air. A guffaw exploded from Badure and even Hasti, shaking her head in exasperation, shared the joke. Chewbacca, blue eyes tearing, slapped Han's shoulder, whereupon the pilot fell sideways, barely able to breathe for laughing.

In the midst of it all, the door swept open.

Bollux was ushered in and the door closed before any of them could do more than gape. In another mo-ment they had congregated around the droid, elbow-

ing one another, their demands for information and
their questions interrupting one another's.

After a few seconds Badure shouted everyone down.
They quieted, realizing he would ask the same questions as they anyway. "What's happened? Who are
those people? What do they want from us?"

Bollux made the strangely human self-effacing
sounds he employed in approaching a delicate subject.
"There's rather a surprising story here. It's somewhat
complicated. You see, long ago, there was—"

"Come on, Bollux!" Han shouted, cutting through
the cybernetic rhetoric, "What are they going to *do*
with us?"

The droid sounded dismayed. "I know it sounds
absurd in this day and age, sir, but unless we can
do something, you're all about to become, er, a human
sacrifice."

☐ XII

"BY which," Skynx said with a forlorn hope, "we may assume you mean *only* humans?"

"Not quite," Bollux admitted. "They're not really sure what you and First Mate Chewbacca are, but they've concluded they have nothing to lose by sacrificing you. They're discussing procedures now."

The Wookiee growled and Skynx's red eyes glazed.

"Bollux, who *are* these people?" Han demanded.

"They call themselves the Survivors, sir. The signal we picked up was a distress call. They're waiting to be picked up. When I asked them why they didn't simply go to the city, they became very vexed and excited; they harbor a great deal of hatred for the other Dellaltians. I gathered that that animosity is tied up with their religion somehow. They are extreme isolationists."

"How did you find all this out?" Badure wanted to know. "Do they speak any Standard?"

"No, sir," the droid replied. "They speak a dialect that was prevalent in this section of space prior to the rise of the Old Republic. It was recorded on a language tape in Skynx's material, and Blue Max had stored it along with other information. Of course, I didn't reveal that Max exists; he translated for me in burst-signals and I conducted the conversation."

"A culture of pre-Republic origins," pondered Skynx, forgetting to be scared.

"Will you forget the homework?" snapped Hasti, then turned again to Bollux. "What's all this about sacrifices? Why us?"

"Because they're waiting to be picked up," said the droid. "They're convinced that life-form termination enhances the effect of their broadcast."

"So *we* stumbled in, a major power boost," mused Han, thinking of all those people who had disappeared in these mountains. "When's the big sendoff?"

"Late tonight, sir; it has something to do with the stars and is accompanied by considerable ritual."

We've got just one trump card left, Han thought, then said, "I think that'll work out just fine."

Their captors wasted no food or drink on them, which Han loudly proclaimed an indication that they had fallen into the hands of a low-class outfit. But they still had plenty of time to question Bollux.

The mountain warren was indeed a large complex, though it apparently housed what Bollux estimated to be no more than one hundred people living in a complicated family-clan group. Asked why he had been separated from them all, the droid could only say that the Survivors appeared to understand what automata were and held them in some awe. They had been adamant about the need to go forward with the sacrifice, but had bowed to his demands that he be permitted to see his companions.

On the details of the sacrifice Bollux was less clear. Ceremonial objects and equipment were being moved to the surface even as they spoke; the sacrifice was to take place on the mock-up landing field. Although the droid had been unable to locate the confiscated weapons, the captives decided that any attempt at escape would have a better chance of success if made on the surface. Han revealed his plan to the others, vague as it was.

"There are a lot of things that could go wrong," Hasti protested.

Han agreed. "The worst of which is getting sacrificed, which will happen anyway. How long until nightfall?"

She consulted her wrist chrono; there were many hours yet. They decided to rest. Chewbacca barked his gameboard move to Han, then settled down for a nap. Badure followed suit.

Han scowled at the Wookiee, whose gameboard move was extremely unconventional. "Just because we're going to be sacrificed, you're playing a reck-

less game now?" The Wookiee flashed his teeth in a
self-satisfied grin.

Skynx appeared to be in deep conversation with
Bollux, using the obscure dialect the Survivors spoke.
Hasti had gone off to commune with her thoughts,
and Han decided not to bother her. He wished urgently
that the group could take some immediate course of
action to dispel any brooding. None was available,
so he settled into that—for him—most difficult of
all tasks, waiting.

The opening of the door brought Han out of a
troubled sleep filled with visions of strangers doing
terrible things to the *Millennium Falcon.*

Then, abruptly, Survivors wearing their extravagant
costumes dashed into the quiet chamber, carrying
glow-rods and weapons, making resistance sheer folly.
Their weapons were a fascinating assortment: ancient
beam-tubes powered by heavy backpacks, antiquated
solid-projectile firearms, and several spring-loaded
harpoon guns of the sort the lake men used. Han's
worst fear, that the Survivors would use their anaes-
thetic gas again and thus preclude any action on their
captives' part, was unrealized. He found himself
breathing easier for that; he had no intention of ending his life passively.

With shouted instructions and gesticulations the
Survivors herded their captives out of the chamber.
They formed a forward and rear guard, keeping
their weapons trained watchfully so there would be
no opportunity for mishap. Chewbacca rumbled angrily through it all and nearly turned on one Survivor,
who had jabbed the Wookiee with a harpoon gun to
hurry him along. Han restrained his friend; all the
other Survivors were out of reach, and there was no
place to hide in the stone corridors. They had no
choice but to move as ordered.

This time Han got a clearer impression of the underground warren. The corridors, like the chamber
in which they had been held, were carefully and precisely cut, arranged along an organized central plan,
their walls, floors, and ceilings fused solid to serve

as support. Thermal plates warmed them, but Han could see no dehumidifying equipment, though he was certain it must exist. Everything implied a technology in excess of what the Survivors seemed capable of fully utilizing. Han was willing to bet these capering primitives did simple maintenance by rote and that the knowledge of the original builders had been lost long ago.

He saw unhelmeted Survivors for the first time, mainbreed humans who, aside from an unusual number of congenital defects, were unremarkable. The prisoners passed heated, well-lit hydroponic layouts. The glow-rods and thermal plates in them made Han wonder about the power source; something suitably ancient, he presumed, perhaps even an atomic pile.

Badure's thoughts had been paralleling his own. "Regression," the old man said. "Maybe the base was built by stranded explorers, or early colonists?"

"That wouldn't explain their unreasoning shunning of the other Dellaltians," Skynx put in. "They must have taken elaborate precautions to avoid notice all this time, even in these desolate—"

He was silenced when a Survivor singled him out with the end of a beam-tube, gesturing with unmistakable fury. Conversation stopped. Han saw that Bollux had been right; the warren had clearly been built for many more people than now occupied it. In some stretches light and heat had been shut down to conserve power or had failed altogether.

They passed a room from which odd, rhythmic sounds issued. For just an instant when he drew even with the doorway, Han had a view of the interior.

Colored lights strobed in the darkness, flashing on the walls and ceiling in arresting swirls and patterns. Someone was chanting in the Survivors' tongue; underscoring the chant was the pulsing of a transonic synthesizer, as much felt as heard.

Han almost stopped short and had to step quickly to keep from being jabbed with a harpoon, thinking, *Hypno-imprinting! Crude version, but completely effective if you catch your subjects early enough. Poor kids.* It explained a lot.

Then they felt cold night air on their faces and their breath crystallized before them. They left the Survivors' warren by a different door than that by which they had entered.

The mockup landing field was a different sight in the night than it had been during the day; it was now a scene of barbaric ceremony. The stars and Dellalt's two moons brightened the sky; glow-rods and streaming torches lit the entire area, reflected by the sides of the dummy aircraft. At the edge of the ritual field, by the steep snowfield that sloped to the valley below, a large cage had been erected, a pyramid of bars, assembled piecemeal. Its door was a thick, solid plate, its lock in the center, inaccessible from within the cage.

Near the cage was a circle of gleaming metal, broader than Han was tall, suspended from a framework, suggesting an enormous gong. It was inscribed with lettering of an unfamiliar type, consisting of whorls and squares alternating with dots and ideographs.

Closer in, toward the center of the light, was a wide metal table, a medi-lab appurtenance of some kind. Near it were piled the prisoners' weapons and other equipment. The implication of the table hit them at once: a sacrificial altar.

Han was ready to make a break then and there; the pyramidal cage seemed firmly anchored to the rock, so sturdy that even Chewbacca's thews wouldn't prevail against it. But the Survivors had been through this procedure before. They were alert and careful, with weapons trained in clear lines of fire. Han noticed that the muzzles and harpoons were pointed toward the captives' legs. If the scheduled sacrificees made any wrong moves, the Survivors could shoot and still not be deprived of their ritual.

This decided the pilot against any immediate action. There was still a chance his plan would work, provided Bollux and Blue Max were flexible enough to adapt to circumstances as they arose. The droid was separated from the rest of them, complying with their captors as Han had instructed him.

The other captives were chivvied to the cage, ushered to the circular door plate that swung open on
oiled hinges. It took every scrap of Han's resolve to
enter the pyramid; once inside he stood there closely
watching the Survivors' preparations.

The strange people were decked out in their finest
garb. Now that he understood a little more about them,
Han could interpret the Survivors' costume. A ground-
crewman's blast-suit had become, over generations, an
insect-eyed getup. Spacesuit speaker grilles had
evolved into pointy-fanged mouths painted on imita-
tion helmets; communication antennae and broadcast
directors were represented by elaborate spikes and
antlers of metal. Back tanks and suit packs were
adorned with symbolic designs and mosaics, while tool
belts were hung with fetishes, amulets, and charms of
all kinds.

The Survivors whirled, leaped, and tootled their
instruments, striking finger chimes and drums. Two
of them beat the great wheel of metal with padded
mallets, the gongings resounding back and forth across
the valley.

With the prisoners' arrival, things began to build
toward a climax. A man mounted a rostrum that had
been set near the altar. A silence fell.

The man wore a uniform festooned with decorations
and braid; his trousers were seamed with golden cloth.
He wore a hat that was slightly small for him, its military brim glittering with giltwork, a broad, flashing me-
dallion riding its high crown. Two aides set a small
stand on the rostrum beside him. It held a thick circle
of transparent material about the size of a mealplate.

"A log-recorder disk!" exclaimed Skynx. The others
competed to ask him if he was sure. "Yes, yes; I've
seen one or two, you know. But the *Queen of Ranroon*'s is back in the treasure vaults, is it not? What
one is that, then?"

No one could answer. The man on the rostrum re-
galed the crowd, delivering loud phrases that they
echoed back to him, applauding, whistling, and stomp-
ing their feet. Flickering torchlight made the scene
seem even more primeval.

"He's saying they've been a good and faithful people, that the proof is there with him on the rostrum, and that the High Command won't forget them," Skynx translated.

Han was amazed. "You understand that garble?"

"I learned it as Bollux did, from the data tapes, a pre-Republic dialect. Can they have been here that long, Captain?"

"Ask the Chamber of Commerce. What's he saying now?"

"He said he's their Mission Commander. And something about mighty forces afoot; the rescue they've been promised will surely come soon. I—something about their generations of steadfastness, and deliverance by this High Command. The crowd keeps chanting 'Our signal will be received.' "

With a final tirade the Mission Commander gestured to the pyramidal cage. Until now Bollux had stood to one side of the proceedings, surrounded by gray-clad, masked Survivors who chanted and rattled prayer clackers at him, descendants of techs entrusted with maintenance of machinery.

But now the droid broke out of their ring, moving quickly to take advantage of the surprise he had caused. He crossed to stand with his back to the pyramid's door. The Survivors who had been about to fetch their first victim for the "transmission" wavered, still awed by the automaton. The droid hadn't been able to secure a weapon, a departure from Han's vague plan, but felt that he could wait no longer to make his move. Even in the rush of events Han wondered about the origin of the Survivors' reverence for mechanicals. Surely there had never been a droid or robot through these mountains before?

The Mission Commander was exhorting his followers. Bollux, his photoreceptors glowing red in the night, slowly opened the halves of his chest plastron. Blue Max, carefully coached by the labor droid, activated his own photoreceptor, playing it across the crowd. Han heard sounds of indrawn breath among the Survivors.

Max switched from optical scanning to holo-projection mode. A cone of light sprang from him; there hovered in the air an image he had recorded off Skynx's tapes, the symbol of Xim the Despot, the grinning death's head with the starburst in each black eye socket. From his vocoder came recorded tech readouts from the tapes in the language of the Survivors.

The crowd drew back, many of them thrusting their thumbs at Bollux to fend off evil. Max put forth more images he had taken from the information Skynx had compiled: an ancient fleet of space battlewagons in flight against the stars; the brilliance of a full-scale engagement with exploding missiles, flaring cannonfire, and probing lasers; battle standards passing in review, displaying unit colors that had been forgotten long ago. The entire time, the droid was surreptitiously edging to the pyramidal cage's door. While the crowd was riveted to Max's performance, Bollux manipulated the door's handle behind his back.

A yell went up from the assembled Survivors just as Bollux succeeded in throwing the bolt on the stubborn lock. Blue Max had projected a holo of the war-robot's cranial turret that Skynx had brought onboard the *Millennium Falcon*. Max held the image, capitalizing on their response, rotating it to show all sides. The Survivors jabbered animatedly among themselves, moving back from the frightening ghost-holo. Bollux stepped away from the cage door.

Max began running through all the other visual information he had stored about Xim's war-robots. Schematics, manual-extracts, records of the ponderous combat machines in motion, closeup details of construction, and full-length views. All the while, Bollux moved slowly forward. Step by step the crowd yielded ground, seemingly hypnotized by Max's projections. In the excitement and poor light nobody noticed that the cage door was now unlocked.

"He may not be able to hold them much longer," Han whispered. Bollux was now at the center of a near-circle of Survivors.

"Time to jump," Badure said.

Han agreed. "Make your way to the edge of the field. Nobody stops for anybody else, understood?"

Hasti, Badure, and even Skynx nodded. Unarmed, they could do little except run from the Survivors. Each individual would be responsible for his own life; stopping to give aid would be suicidal and expected of no one.

Han swung the door open slowly and stepped through. Shouting, gesticulating Survivors were still occupied with Bollux. The Mission Commander had left his rostrum to try to make his way through the crowd to Bollux, but was having trouble making headway through the press of his own people. Han waited while the others emerged.

Chewbacca slipped through the door and moved off like a shadow. Badure moved with less agility, then Hasti. Skynx exited and set off at once for the edge of the field. Low to the ground, he was nearly impossible to see. The Ruurian didn't pause or look back; he adhered to Han's directions completely, having acquired some of the necessary makeup of an adventurer. Han moved around the end of the cage to bring up the rear. He nearly backed into Hasti. "Where's Badure?" she mouthed silently.

They couldn't spot him at first, then made out the old man as he nonchalantly strolled around the edge of the crowd, heading for the abandoned altar where the weapons lay. No one paid him any heed; all of them were transfixed by Max's holos of a war-robot being put through its paces, firing weapons, and lumbering through basic infantry tactics.

"He's going for the guns," Han whispered. Chewbacca, who had also paused, stood with them, watching the old man's progress.

"We can't help him now; he either makes it or not. We'll wait at the edge of the field as long as we can." He didn't know if he was happy Badure was trying for their weapons, feeling naked and helpless without his blaster, or dismayed that the old man was risking his life.

Just then a Survivor sentry, coming in off his post, stepped out of the darkness and nearly stumbled over Skynx. The Ruurian chirped in fear and went into reverse. The guard's eyes bulged in amazement at the woolly, many-legged creature, then he fumbled for the flame-rifle at his shoulder, crying out an alarm.

A shaggy arm reached out and the weapon was snatched from his hands. Chewbacca's fist shot through the air and the guard was lifted, stretched out stiff as a post, to fall on the landing field, his left foot quivering.

People on the fringe of the crowd had heard the guard and repeated the alarm. Heads turned; in a moment the shout was taken up by many voices. Han ran, took the bell-mouthed flame-rifle, and slewed it in a wide, horizontal arc. A wash of orange fire streamed over the heads of the crowd. Survivors dropped to the ground, grabbing for their weapons and screaming conflicting orders at one another. Han could hear the shrieking Mission Commander trying futilely to bring order out of chaos.

Badure, having reached the altar, was out of the crowd's immediate line of sight. He shouldered Chewbacca's bowcaster and bandoleer of ammunition and began tucking weapons into his belt.

Shots were now being pegged across the field at them. "Keep out of the way!" hollered Han, elbowing Chewbacca behind him. He backed slowly, covering the withdrawal and creating a diversion for Badure. He directed his discharges into the ground between himself and the massed Survivors, making puddles of fire to spoil their aim and sending intermittent streamers of flame over them to force their heads down. A line of tracer bullets chewed up the field a meter or two to his right, and a pale particle beam barely missed his head.

The escapees needed cover badly, but their section of the field was open and offered none. Chewbacca, with sudden inspiration, ran for the gong and, back and arm muscles swelling with effort, lifted it from its support hooks, his widespread arms grabbing it by two carrying handles welded to its back.

The slugs, beams, and flames of the firefight dissected the air. The Survivors' shots were gaining in accuracy, though they weren't used to such a pitched battle. Badure, running in a low crouch to work his way back to his companions, was spotted by the crowd. Somebody let fly with an old rocket pistol, blowing up a clot of stone in his path. In a frantic effort to change course, Badure lost his balance, and Survivors' shots began to converge on him.

Chewbacca grounded the gong in front of Han as he and the others took shelter behind it. Projectile and energy weapons splashed and ricochetted from the shield; whatever the gong was made of, it was very durable material.

Han blazed away at the Survivors to keep them from pressing the attack against Badure. He had been spending the flame-rifle's ammo recklessly and knew he might soon find himself defenseless. Badure, struggling to rise, was having trouble. The Survivors' aim was zeroing in on him now, and he returned the fire as well as he could.

I warned him, thought Han. *Life-Debt or no, it's everyone for himself.* He had trouble selling the idea to himself, though.

Then the decision was taken from him. Issuing a deafening Wookiee battle cry, Chewbacca moved off, holding up the gong to protect himself. Han looked back and saw that Hasti and Skynx were watching him. The girl, he thought, would surely run to help Badure if he didn't.

"Don't just stand there," he snarled. "Get to cover!" He gave her a shove toward the edge of the field and dashed off the other way, laying down heavy fire as he sprinted, zig-zagging after the Wookiee.

"You crazy fur-face!" he roared at his first mate when he had caught up to him. "What're you doing, playing captain again?" Chewbacca took a moment from angling and maneuvering the gong for an irritated, explanatory growl.

"Life-Debt?" Han exploded, dodging around his friend into the open to snap off a pair of quick shots. "And who pays up if you lose us *ours?*"

But he maintained his fire, sideskipping along behind the straining, gong-toting Wookiee and bounding from cover to either side of him to get off a shot or two. Flames lit the scene, and the air was smoky and hot from the firefight. The flame-rifle's discharges were growing weaker, and its range was decreasing.

Skirting a section of field torn and ruptured by the battle, they finally reached Badure, who was pressed down flat on the ground, shooting with the pair of long-barreled power pistols. Chewbacca heaved the gong between the old man and the oncoming shots. Han coaxed a last feeble flicker from the flame-rifle, then threw it aside. Dropping to one knee, he helped Badure up. "Last bus is leaving now, Lieutenant-commander."

"I'll take a one-way on that," panted Badure, adding, "glad you could make it, boys."

Han snagged his own blaster from Badure's belt, and a sudden confidence steadied him. He stepped into the clear, crouched low, and let off a series of quick shots. Two Survivor marksmen who had been taking careful aim with heavy-particle beamers fell away in different directions, their wounds smoking.

Han ducked back, waited a beat, then stepped into the open again on the same side of the gong, eluding the aim of those who had been waiting to see him emerge on the opposite side. His bolts dropped two more enemies from the ragged firing line. But Survivor flankers could be seen in the wavering light, fanning out to either side in an effort to cut off retreat.

"Let's jump!" Han cried. Chewbacca began back-pedaling, still holding the gong, and headed for the field's edge as Badure and Han kept up the most intense fire they could, pinning down the Survivors facing them and impeding the flankers. Their energy weapons lit the night, answered by bullets, blaster bolts, needles, harpoons, particle beams, and gushes of flame. Han occasionally assisted the Wookiee's progress with a judicious shove.

Someone came toward them. Badure nearly burned the silhouetted form before Han batted the power pistol aside. "Bollux! Over here!"

The droid somehow made it to the gong's cover; they withdrew step by hotly contended step. A group of Survivor flankers was nearly in position to enfilade them, crouching by the antenna mast. Badure held both long-barreled weapons up side by side and fired at the flankers. Men fell and the instrument shorted out; the mast's power supply was drained in a swirl of energy, and the mast fell, wreathed in crackling discharges. It crashed into the rostrum and rostrum, frame, and log-recorder disk went up in flames.

Han heard his name called. Skynx and Hasti crouched at the edge of the field. Firing and scrambling, the others joined them.

"We can't retreat down that snowfield; it's too steep," Hasti declared, "and even Chewbacca couldn't carry that gong down. We'd make perfect targets out there."

Han dealt out a few more shots, pondering her reasoning and their lack of alternatives. Then Chewbacca, surveying the situation, barked a quick scheme to him.

"Partner, you *are* crazy," Han exclaimed, not without a certain respect. But he saw no nonfatal alternative. "What's keeping us?" He pulled the others closer and explained the plan. They readied themselves, having no time for fear or doubts.

Then Han yelled. "Chewie! Go!" The Wookiee backpedaled to the edge of the field, whirled, stooped, and laid the concave gong down, its curved surface indenting the hard, icy snowfield. Han fired furiously.

Badure dropped awkwardly onto the gong and grabbed a carrying handle. Bollux climbed onto the opposite side of the rim, locking servo-grips onto two more handles. Skynx swarmed aboard and clung tightly around the droid's neck, antennae flailing. Hasti braced herself next to Badure, and Chewbacca had to brace his broad feet in the snow at the tug of the gong's weight.

Han still stood, keeping up a heavy volume of fire. He shouted, "I'll pile on last!"

Chewbacca didn't take time to argue; he swept out one long arm, gathered his friend in like a child, and threw himself onto the gong. Shots from the Survivor flankers crisscrossed overhead. The Wookiee's impetus and weight gave them a quick start.

The gong gathered speed, spinning and sliding as it

cut along the icy slope. Chewbacca lifted his head and uttered a foghorn-like hoot of elation, to which Skynx added a *"Wee-ee hee-ee!"*

The gong tilted and rotated to the left as it swished across the snow. Chewbacca threw his weight the other way; they bounced and slid on a fairly even keel for a few seconds, then hit a small rock outcropping in the snowfield.

They were airborne, all hands seeking a grip and flailing to stay aboard; to fall from the gong now and slide the rest of the way without protection would mean severe laceration by ice shards and shattered bones from the hardened patches and rocks.

They came down again with a breath-stealing jolt; everyone, miraculously, contrived to cling to the bucking, jarring gong. Han grabbed Hasti, who, in helping Badure, had nearly lost her own grip. The *Falcon's* master encircled her waist with his free arm while she clenched a handful of Badure's flight jacket. Badure, in turn, had locked legs with Chewbacca, helping the Wookiee steer by leaning and tugging at the handles. Chewbacca, like the others, could barely see; their headlong speed through the icy air had stung everyone's eyes to tears and was numbing their exposed skin.

In leaning abruptly to the side, the Wookiee succeeded in guiding their mad descent around a prow of stone that would have smashed them all, but in the process he lost his balance. Bollux quickly shifted his central torsional member and secured his legs around the *Falcon's* first officer's.

Badure held onto Chewbacca, too, reaching out with a free hand to help steady the Wookiee. But in doing so he saw he was about to lose Chewbacca's bowcaster and bandoleer. He cried out, his words stolen instantly by the wind, but Han was busy clinging to a handle and hanging onto Hasti and she to Badure, while Badure and Bollux were committed to keeping Chewbacca aboard. Meanwhile, the Wookiee devoted all his attention to what could only in the most ludicrous sense be termed "steering."

And so Skynx, facing the fact that only he was free

to act, released his grip on the droid with all but his last set of limbs. He was dragged around at once, very nearly snapped like a whip, reaching with his free extremities. Just as Badure's scrabbling efforts to hang onto the bowcaster failed, Skynx got close enough to grasp the weapon and was abruptly thrown in the other direction as the gong changed course again.

The small Ruurian now clung to his only mainstay, Bollux, by the digits of his lowermost limbs, which clenched precariously on the droid's shoulder pauldron. But he determinedly hung onto the weapon and ammunition, knowing they might be needed badly and that there was no one to catch them if he failed. With each bump and rotation of the gong, Skynx felt his grip loosening, but he hugged his burden resolutely. One by one, he began to find purchase for his other limbs. Chewbacca felt him fumbling, shifted his leg as much as he was able, and Skynx managed to fasten two sets of limbs to the Wookiee's thick knee.

They were at the steepest part of the insane plunge, shearing through the snowfield, rocking in furrows, and smashing out of depressions in the surface. Several times Han saw energy beams of various hues register hits in the snow, but always far wide of their mark. *As targets go, we must be pretty fast and furious.*

He clung doggedly, fingers, ears, and face numbed by the cold, eyes streaming a constant flow of tears. "My fingers are slipping!" cried Hasti with unmasked fear. "I can't feel them."

Han knew with a sense of utter futility that he could do little to help her. He gripped her as tightly as he could, hoping that his frozen fingers would hold.

Badure yelled. "We're slowing down!" Chewbacca bellowed pure joy. Hasti began to half-laugh, half-sob.

The gong had reached a gentler portion of the slope close to the foot of the snowfield and was losing speed moment by moment. The bumps and jolts became less dramatic, the spinning less pronounced. In seconds they were coasting.

"An excellent job, First Mate Chewbacca," Bollux was saying, when suddenly the gong's rim hit a slab of rock that lifted it into the air like a jump ramp. Frozen hands, servo-grips, Ruurian digits, and Wookiee toes, all lost their final struggle. The gong threw them free. Human bodies, the tubular Skynx, a yeowling Chewbacca, and gleaming Bollux sailed through the air on assorted trajectories, cartwheeling, tumbling, spinning —and falling.

☐ XIII

HAN heard the whine of servo-motors over the moan of wind. From where he lay, mostly buried by the mound of snow he had scraped up on his landing approach, he could see Bollux draped belly-up over a low snowbank. The halves of the droid's chest plastron opened up and outward.

Blue Max's vocoder blustered. "Hey! Let's get moving; we're not out of it yet!"

A drift to Han's right sloughed and erupted. Chewbacca appeared, spitting out snow and rumbling an acid remark to the diminutive computer module.

"No, he's right," Han groaned to his partner. He raised himself on unsteady arms and gazed up the slope, foggily curious about whether his head was actually going to fall off or if it simply felt that way. A bobbing column of lights was wending its way down the snowfield from the Survivors' base. Their former captors were in hot pursuit.

"The short circuit's right on the money, folks; everybody up!" Han thrashed and floundered in the snow for a moment, then pulled himself to his feet and began beating his hands together to bring some sensation back.

Hasti was also struggling up. Han caught her hand and pulled her to her feet. She ran over to see to Badure. Chewbacca had just reclaimed his bowcaster and bandoleer from Skynx, whom he had dug free. The Wookiee growled his gratitude, patting and stroking the Ruurian's woolly back in a gruff gesture of thanks.

Hasti was chafing Badure's hands and wrists, trying to get him upright. Han moved to help and saw that the tip of the old man's nose and patches on his cheeks were whitened.

"He's getting frostbite. On deck, Trooper; time to depart the area." They pulled him up. Meanwhile, with Chewbacca's help, Bollux was once more upright.

Counting heads before striking off, Han spied Skynx bent over the gong, which had fallen face up, a flattened dome in the snow. The Ruurian was making minute examination of the whorls and patterns on the ancient metal, laboring to see in the light of moons and stars. When Han called him, the academician yelled back. "I think you'd better see this first, Captain."

They all gathered around him. His small digits traced the raised characters. "I thought I recognized these when I first saw this object, but I was too hurried to study them. All these," a splay of digits indicated groups of characters, "are technical notations and operating instructions. They have to do with pressure equalization and fastening procedures."

"Then it comes from a hatch," Badure concluded, his muffled voice coming through hands cupped to thaw out his cheeks and nose. "Some kind of decorative facing off an airlock hatch, a big one."

Skynx agreed. "A peculiar and rather ostentatious appointment, but that is the case. Those several larger characters there in the center give the vessel's name." He turned bulbous red eyes to them. "It's the *Queen of Ranroon!*"

In the middle of a tumult of voices—human, nonhuman, and electronic—Han stood imagining the treasure of entire worlds. Though cold, near exhaustion, pursued, and starved, he suddenly found himself charged with limitless energy and a dramatic determination to live and to claim the *Queen's* wealth.

They were interrupted. Han's thoughts and the confused conversations springing from Skynx's revelation were cut short by a long note sounding in the night, a wail from a hunting horn or other signaling device.

That brought them all up short. The bobbing lights of the pursuing Survivors' column were now well down the slope. Now and then one would drop from the line and disappear as its bearer lost footing on the treacherous snowfield and fell tumbling.

Led by Han, the escapees set out in a staggering string, helping one another as well as they could; fortunately, the snow wasn't very deep. They reached down to scoop up handfuls of the stuff to melt in their mouths, trying to relieve the dehydration of their captivity. Beating his gloved hands together, Han considered what the hatch cover might mean. Were the Survivors guarding Xim's treasure in their mountain warren? What had become of the *Queen of Ranroon?*

Hasti caught up to him in the struggling line of march. "Solo, I've been doing some thinking. The congregation back there isn't just tooting their horns to hear the echoes and let us know they're coming. I think they have patrols out and are calling the forces out on us."

He stopped, deriding himself for having been preoccupied with the treasure. Hasti repeated her reasoning to the others. "We're not too far from the snow line," Badure observed. "Perhaps that's the limit to their territory."

Han shook his head. "We messed up church for them and left quite a few of them in some pain. They're coming for blood and they won't stop just because the snow does. We'd better take up a better formation. Chewie, walk the point."

The Wookiee padded off quietly; cold and snow didn't bother him. Protected by his thick pelt, he slipped off, keeping to the cover of the increasingly frequent rocks and boulders. The others followed more slowly in his wake, slowed because they were bereft of his giant, supportive strength.

But within minutes the Wookiee was back to draw them down into the cover of a particularly large boulder and tell Han, in quick gutterals, what he had encountered.

"There're more of them, coming up this way," Han translated. "Chewie thinks we can hide here and wait them out. When they're past, we go on. Still and quiet, everybody."

They waited for oppressive minutes, straining to make no noise, no shift of position or other movement that might betray them. Han slowly turned his head to check the progress of the Survivors from their base. The lights had made their way to the gentler part of the slope and fanned out for a ground search.

There was a slight sound, the smallest movement of rock and crunch of ice. Everyone tensed. A shape moved stealthily into view, keeping to available cover. The approaching Survivor was uncostumed but wore a hood and heavy clothing. The scout's head turned slowly, searching the area carefully as he went. Moments later another sentinel appeared, farther across the valley on a parallel course.

Han thought he understood. The valley widened abruptly from here, and a few sentries, farther along, might not be able to stop the escapees from getting past. The sentries kept moving warily. When they were well past the escapees' position, Han—using hand-touches to alert his companions and dictate the order of march—slipped out from behind the boulder. The servo-motors of Bollux's body were smooth and quiet, but sounded unbearably loud to Han. He could only hope the sound didn't carry over the wind and other noises in the night.

They had wound their way among the rocks for another half kilometer and gotten out of sght of the snowfield, and Han had just begun to let himself believe they were clear, when a yellow heatbeam flashed out of the night. It scored on a rock two meters to Bollux's right, throwing up sparks and globs of molten mineral.

Chill, shivers, frozen feet, and caution were forgotten. Everybody scattered for cover. Hasti brought her disruptor pistol up for a return shot but Han whispered, "Don't! He'll pick up your position from the flash. Anybody see where the shot came from?" Nobody had. "Then, sit still. When he fires again, we'll nail him. Aim for the point of origin."

"Solo, we haven't got time to sit here!" Hasti rasped fiercely.

"Then start tunneling," he suggested.

But instead she groped, found a stone that fit her palm, and heaved it. It clattered among the loose rocks. Another heatbeam flashed yellow from the shadows at the side of the valley.

Han fired instantly and kept on firing. The others, slower than he, joined a moment later with a torrent of blaster, power pistol, disruptor, and bowcaster shots.

"Hold it, hold it," Han ordered. "I think we got him."

"Do we move on?" asked Badure.

Han didn't think the light and reports of the shots would have been detectable back on the slopes. "Not yet. We have to be sure we won't get backshot. Besides, I saw a gleam of metal where the heatbeams came from. Maybe there's a vehicle there, or some supplies." He shivered from the mountain air. "Anything'd be a help."

"Then someone must investigate," Skynx declared and was away before anybody could stop him, flowing between the rocks with his antennae held low, nearly impossible to see. *I'll have to warn him about those heroics*, Han thought, *he's come a long way.* To break the tense silence, he whispered to Badure, "See what happens? First you go off medal-chasing to get our weapons back and now Skynx figures he's the valiant warrior."

The old man chuckled softly. "The guns came in handy, didn't they? Besides, it gave Chewbacca a chance to pay back his Life-Debt."

Han blinked. "That's right. Hey, what do you mean Chewbacca? We *both* came back for you!" Badure only laughed.

Just then Skynx called excitedly, "Captain! Over here!" They went, slipping and stumbling with haste but still keeping low. They came to an overhang of rock, having to duck to pass under it. From the black regions within issued Skynx's voice. "I found a glow-rod, Captain Solo. I'll turn up the rheostat a bit." A faint glimmer showed them the Ruurian's face.

He had found a low, wide cave that reached in farther than they could see. The body of the single sentry was sprawled in death, hit by several of their blasts. But what excited Skynx was what had been under guard there.

"Look, a cargo lifter!" Han took the glow-rod. "Hover-raft of some kind." He climbed into the open cockpit of the flatbed aircraft. "Looks like it was on down time; there're a lot of burned-out components on the floorboards, and the control-panel covers are still off."

He brightened the glow-rod. There were two more hover-rafts nearby, access panels open, gutted and cannibalized for the parts that had gone to repair the first. Han slid the notched hover bar down; the craft rose a bit.

He flicked controls; the board was clear. "Hop in; my meter's running."

They rushed to comply, ducking to keep from bumping heads on the cave ceiling. With one foot on a mounting step, Badure paused. "What was that?"

They all heard it—the sounds of running, voices, and the clatter of weapons. "Hot pursuit," answered Han. "No time to punch tickets, folks: stay gripped!"

He rammed up the impeller control, red-zoning the engine. The hover-raft shot out of the cave, nearly losing Bollux, who had been in the process of boarding. Badure and Chewbacca dragged him aboard.

The Survivors were closer than Han had thought; they had assumed positions around the cave and were closing in on it. The hover-raft zoomed from the cave near ground level, engines complaining. One or two Survivors had the presence of mind to shoot as the raft flashed by, but most either stood frozen or sought a lower elevation to keep from being run down. The few shots went wild, and Hasti put out a few rounds at random to keep the Survivors' heads down. The raft tore through a wide arc and headed down the valley.

"Where to, citizens?" Han grinned.

"Just turn on the heaters!" yelled Hasti.

The valley widened quickly, then gave way down to an open plain carpeted with bobbing, spindly amber grass. The hover-raft was equipped with rudimentary navigational gear. Han set a course for J'uoch's mining camp. Not wanting to use the raft's running lights, he cut his speed back and peered through the windshield, thankful it was a bright night.

The wind of their passage snatched the warmth out of the heater grids. Hasti discovered a folded tarp in one corner of the cargo bed and pulled at it, but stopped and called to the others. "Look at what they had onboard!"

Han couldn't turn from his steering, but Chewbacca, sitting next to him, pulled a handful of the tarp over the back of the driver's seat. Carefully fastened to the tarp were strands of plastic, meticulously fashioned to look like the amber grass of the plains. A camouflage cover.

"This crate comes equipped with an aerial-sensor, too," Han noted. "With a little warning and time to cover up, this thing would be just about impossible to spot without first-rate equipment." And the cave had been big enough to hold more rafts like this one. But that left the question of how a group of primitives like the Survivors, on a back-eddy planet like Dellalt, had set up an operation like this.

Han slowed just enough for Chewbacca to wrestle the collapsible canopy into place. They crowded onto the short couches of the cramped pilot-passenger compartment, lit by the glow of the dashboard instruments and Bollux's photoreceptors. Outside, the moons and stars lit a sea of waving grassland as it blurred under the raft's darkened bow. Eventually the heaters made some headway, and Han opened his flight jacket.

Badure sighed. "If that was the *Queen*'s log-recorder disk back there, we can write it off. The antenna mast destroyed it completely."

Han posed the question: "But how did the Survivors get it in the first place? I thought it was back in the vaults."

"They were talking like it's been theirs all along," Hasti put in, shifting in a futile attempt to find more room between Bollux and Badure in the back seat.

Skynx, in his best classroom voice, chimed in. "The facts, as we know them, are as follows. Lanni somehow obtained the log-recorder disk and deposited it in a lockbox in the vaults. She evinced an interest in the mountains. J'uoch discovered her secret, or some part of it, and killed Lanni in trying to obtain the disk. And, here were the Survivors with either the same disk or one identical to it.

"Now, Lanni was a pilot, flying freight and operational missions, isn't that right? Suppose she happened to be airborne when the Survivors were holding one of their outdoor ceremonies, and either traced their signal or saw the light?"

Han nodded. "She could've landed somewhere, scouted, and bagged the log-recorder!" He trimmed the craft and corrected its course a bit.

Hasti agreed. "She could have. Dad taught her to fly, and a lot about wilderness survival and reconnaissance."

Badure picked up the thread. "So she put the disk in the lockbox and stopped off across the lake to see if she could detect a bounce or signal leakage or find out anything about the Survivors' base, or if she'd stirred them up. I bet the treasure's back there under the mountain."

They rode in silence for a time. Then Han spoke: "That would only leave two questions: how to get the *Falcon* back . . . and how to spend all that money."

Han's best efforts failed to nurse much speed from the antiquated raft. He kept the airwatch sensor on, depressed as low to the horizon astern as possible, but he detected no pursuit. He was still unsatisfied, having come up with no conclusions as to what the Survivors had been doing with those cargo craft, what the hatch face off the *Queen of Ranroon* actually meant, or how it was all connected with the treasure.

Dellalt's sun set off a purple dawn; grassland disappeared under the hover-raft's bow. They had nearly crossed the basin of grassland formed by a curve in the mountain range and were bearing toward the mining camp when Bollux leaned over the driver's seat and said, "Captain, I've been making communication monitoring sweeps as you ordered, listening for activity on the Survivors' frequency."

Han immediately became anxious. "Are they on the air?"

"No," answered the droid. "After all, their antenna mast was destroyed. But I also checked other frequencies mentioned in Skynx's tapes, and I've found something peculiar. There are transmissions on a very unusual setting coming from the direction of the campsite. They're odd because, although I can't pick them up clearly, they appear to be cyber-command signals."

Han's brow furrowed. Automata-command signals? "Mining equipment?" he asked the droid.

"No," answered Bollux. "These aren't the usual heavy-equipment patterns or industrial signals."

Badure turned the raft's commo rig to the setting Bollux had been monitoring but was unable to pick up anything clearly. Taking a bearing from the droid, Han changed course minutely and made a slow approach toward the mountains. Setting the airwatch sensor to full-scan, he readied Chewbacca and the others to pull the camouflage tarp over the raft at a moment's notice.

He came in slowly, taking his direction from the droid. They had already walked into one trap by investigating signals and, though it was important that they find out what these new ones meant, Han had no intention of being ambushed a second time. He lowered the raft's lift factor until it was bending the grass down, barely clearing the ground.

"Signals strengthening, Captain," advised Bollux.

They were approaching a rise in the plains, a ripple in the landscape preliminary to the sloping of the mountains. Han settled the hover-raft in behind the rise and got out of the craft. Parting the grass delicately, he and Chewbacca belly-crawled to the crest to have a look.

Less than a kilometer away the foothills began. Han squinted through his blaster's scope. "There's something down there, where that gully comes down to the plain."

The Wookiee agreed. They withdrew with care and told the others what they had seen. Sunrise was near.

"Skynx and Hasti, take lookout on the rise," Han directed. "Bollux and Badure, guard the raft. Chewie and I will move in; you all know the signal system. If you have to get out, at least you've got a boat now." None of them made any objections, though Hasti looked as if she wanted to.

The *Millennium Falcon*'s captain and first mate split off to the right and left of the rise, moving stealthily through the tall, amber grass, each of them keeping careful count in his mind. They had worked together so often that they automatically orchestrated their moves, without benefit of chrono or signal.

Han swept left, approaching the anomaly in the terrain that had attracted his attention. As he had thought, the lumps at the base of the foothills were a cluster of camouflage covers, a little too sudden and consolidated to be a part of the landscape. He saw no sentries or patrols, no surveillance of any kind, and so changed course to his right.

He heard something in the grass that might have been a small insect's buzz; the sound scarcely traveled a few meters. Han assumed his partner's signal had been sounding for a while.

He homed to it, parted a tuft of grass, and met his copilot with a grin. They talked in quick hand-motions; Chewbacca's recon had yielded the same results as Han's—with one addition: there was a guard, evidently a Survivor, walking a slow post. They made their plan and moved forward again. Han's first inclination was to use the stun-gun carried by Badure, but there was too much chance that someone would hear the discharge or see the blue light of the shot.

The sentry was dressed in common Dellaltian mode rather than in Survivor garb. He strolled along his circuit carelessly, armed with a Kell Mark II Heavy Assault Rifle. He carried the Kell at a sloppy shoulder angle. Like sentries in most of the places Han had ever seen, the man was convinced that nothing would happen and that he was walking guard for no good reason. He sauntered past, thinking thoughts of no great consequence—which was just as well. Those idle thoughts were dispelled a moment later when a hulking shape rose out of the grass behind him and expertly tapped him behind the ear with a bowcaster butt. The guard fell face-first into the grass.

Han retrieved the heavy-assault rifle, and the two partners made a hasty scout of the area. There were no more guards, but the thing that had attracted Han's attention through the blaster scope proved most interesting. All manner of ground-effect surface vehicles, all of them cargo models, were gathered there under camouflage covers, secured. A quick series of random checks revealed no cargo aboard any of them.

"What'd they need twenty flatbeds for?" Han wondered aloud as he waved his companions forward. "Plus two or three back at the mountain base?"

The others came up behind them. Badure explained that they had secured the stolen hover-raft with its own camouflage cover, behind the rise. They helped Han and Chewbacca in a precautionary smashing of the fleet's communication equipment. None of them could come up with a plausible reason for the strange gathering of craft either.

"There's a gully leading up into the foothills," Han said, jerking his thumb. "How far are we from J'uoch's mining camp?"

"Straight up that way," Hasti told him, indicating the gully. "We can work our way along a few ridge lines and we'll be there. Or, we could go along the valley floors and washes."

Han hefted the Kell rifle. "Let's move out now; we'll all go. I don't want to leave anybody behind in case we get a break and get the *Falcon* back; we can raise ship right away."

They started into the foothills, eyes darting nervously for any sign of ambush. Bollux, monitoring, picked up no evidence of sensors. The gully's floor had been sluiced by rains down to hard stone, scored and chewed as if heavy equipment had passed over it. They had seen no tracks or tread marks on the plain, but the resilient grass probably wouldn't have held them.

Bollux reported that the automata-command signals were much stronger now. "They're repetitive," the droid informed them, "as if someone is running the same test sequence over and over."

The gully cut through the first two ridges and gave out on the next, the highest they had reached. The ground here was all rock, still showing signs of the passage of what Han assumed to be machinery. That the Survivors had some special interest in J'uoch's camp was obvious; it remained to be seen if it had to do with the treasure. But uppermost in Han's mind was recovery of the *Millennium Falcon.*

They topped the ridge, advancing at a low crawl, to look down into the valley below. Hasti gasped, as did Skynx with a sound like a subdued hiccup. Bollux gazed without comment, less surprised than the others. Han's and Chewbacca's mouths hung open, and Badure whispered, "By the Maker!"

Now the fleet of cargo craft, the marks on the stone gully floor, the gist of the Survivors' ceremony—even the huge chamber in which they had been imprisoned —all made sense. Those monolithic stone slabs set deep in the mountain warren weren't tables, runways, or partitions.

They were benches.

And below were gathered the occupants that sat on those benches, at least a thousand of the bulky war-robots built at the command of Xim the Despot. They stood immobile, broad and impassive, mightily armored—man-shaped battle machines half again Han's height. They gleamed with a mirror-bright finish designed to reflect laser weaponry. Survivors moved among them with testing equipment, running the checks Bollux had detected.

"These are the ones!" Skynx whispered gleefully. "The thousand guardians Xim set onboard the *Queen of Ranroon* to look after his treasure. I wonder how many trips it took to ferry them all out here? And what are they here for?"

"The only possible reason's over there," replied Hasti, gesturing with her chin, raising up on her elbows. From their vantage point they could see J'uoch's mining camp, which straddled two sides of a great crevasse. The barracks, shops, and storage buildings were on one side, the kilometers-wide mining-operations site on the other, the two connected by a massive trestle bridge left from old Dellaltian mining efforts. The camp seemed to be operating as usual, its heavy equipment tearing away at the ground.

And on the side of the site, Han saw something that nearly made him whoop out loud. He pounded the Wookiee's shoulder, pointing. There, the *Millennium Falcon* sat on her triangle of landing gear. The starship seemed intact and operational.

But she won't be, Han caught himself up short, *if those groundpounders of Xim's get at her.*

At that moment there was a flurry of activity among the Survivors below. Their testing sequences were done. They scurried out from among the irregularly placed robots and gathered at a gleaming golden podium that had been set up on one side of the valley. A transmission horn projected from the podium, which was adorned with Xim's death's-head emblem. The Survivor on the podium touched a control.

Every war-robot on the valley floor straightened to alertness, squaring shoulders, coming to stiff, straddle-legged attention. Cranial turrets swung; optical pickups came to bear on the podium. The Survivor on the podium spoke.

"He's calling the Corps Commander forward," Skynx explained in a muted voice.

"I know that man on the podium," Hasti whispered slowly. Then more quickly, "I recognize the white blaze in his hair. He's the assistant to the steward of the treasure vaults!"

From the massed robots stepped their leader, identical to the others in his corps but for a golden insignia glittering on his breastplate. His rigid, weighty tread shook the ground, the epitome of military precision, his movements revealing immense power. He halted before the podium. From his aged vocoder came a deep, resonant question. Skynx translated in whispers.

"What do you require of the Guardian Corps?" the machine intoned.

"That with which you were entrusted is now in jeopardy," answered the Survivor on the podium, the steward's assistant.

"What do you require of the Guardian Corps?" repeated the robot, uninterested in details.

The Survivor pointed. "Follow the gully trail as we've marked it for you. It will bring you to your enemies. Destroy all that you find there. Kill everyone you encounter."

The armored head regarded him for a moment, as if in doubt, then replied: "You occupy the control platform; the Guardian Corps will obey. We will pass in review, as programmed, then go forth." The Corps Commander's cranial turrets rotated as he issued the squeals of his signalry.

The war-robots began moving, forming an irregular line, moving just as their commander had. Without cadence or formation, they grouped to one side of the podium. But as they passed it, the transmission horn's command circuitry automatically directed them to assume their review mode. From a massed group, they separated into ranks and files as they passed the podium, ten abreast, heavy feet rising and falling in step. With their Corps Commander at their head, the thousand war-robots marched, completing a circuit of the little valley.

Even the Survivors were hypnotized by it; the sight of their ancient charges walking again was nothing less than magical to them. Metal feet beat the canyon floor; arms as thick as a man's waist swung in unison. Han wondered if J'uoch's people wouldn't be able to hear their approach even over the sound of mining operations.

At some unseen signal from their Corps Commander, the robots stopped. The commander came around to face the podium with a rocking motion. From his vocoder boomed the words: "We are ready."

The Survivor on the podium instructed the robots to stand fast for a time. "We go now to a vantage point, from which we will observe your attack. When we are in place you may proceed against the enemy." He and the other Survivors hurried off to watch the carnage. Presently the air was still, the war-robots waiting patiently, the only sound the distant buzz of the mining camp.

"We've got to get to the camp first," Han declared as they drew back from the ridge and got to their feet.

"Are you completely vacuum-happy?" Hasti wanted to know. "We'll get there just in time to go through the meat-grinder!"

"Not if we hurry. Those windup soldiers down there will have to go the long way around; we can run the ridge line if we're careful and get there first. The *Falcon*'s our only way off this mud-ball; if we can't get to her, we're going to have to tip J'uoch that the robots are on their way, or they'll rip my ship apart."

He wished he could figure out why the Survivors were intent on destroying the mining camp and slaughtering its personnel. "Everyone keep up. I'll go first, then Hasti, Skynx, Badure, Bollux, and Chewie on rearguard."

Han put the heavy-assault rifle across his shoulders and set off, the others falling into their assigned places. But when Chewbacca beckoned Bollux, the labor droid hesitated. "I'm afraid I'm not functioning up to specifications, First Mate Chewbacca. I'll have to come along as best I can."

The Wookiee was torn by indecision for a moment, then trotted off after the rest, making it clear with hand motions and growls that Bollux was to come along as quickly as he could. The droid watched Chewbacca disappear from view, then opened his chest plastron so that he and Blue Max could speak in vocal-normal mode, as they preferred.

"Now, my friend," he drawled to the little computer module, "perhaps you'll explain why you wanted us to stay behind. I practically had to lie to First Mate Chewbacca to do it; we may very well be left behind."

Max, who had taken in the situation via direct

linkage with Bollux, answered simply. "I know how to stop them. The war-robots, I mean; but we'd have to destroy them all to do it. We needed time to talk it over, Bollux."

And Blue Max related the plan he had conceived. The labor droid responded even more slowly than usual. "Why didn't you mention this before, when Captain Solo was here?"

"Because I didn't want him to decide! Those robots are doing what they were built to do, just like we are. Is that any reason to obliterate them? I wasn't even sure I should tell you; I didn't want you to blow your primary stacks in a decisional malfunction. Wait; what're you doing?"

The labor droid's chest plastron was swinging shut as he toed the edge of the ridge. "Seeking alternatives," he explained, stepping off.

Bollux slid and stumbled and plowed his way down the slope to the valley floor, working with heavy-duty suspension of arms and legs to keep from being damaged. At last he came to an awkward stop at the bottom amid a minor avalanche. Standing erect, he approached the war-robots, who waited in their gleaming, exact formation.

The Corps Commander's cranial turret rotated at Bollux's advance. A great arm swung up, weapons-apertures opening. "Halt. Identify or be destroyed."

Bollux replied with the recognition codes and authentication signals he had learned from Skynx's ancient tapes and technical records. The Corps Commander studied him for a moment, debating whether this strange machine ought to be obliterated, recognition codes or no. But the war-robots' deliberative circuitry was limited. The weapon-arm lowered again. "Accepted. State your purpose."

Bollux, with no formal diplomatic programming to draw upon and only his experience to guide him, began hesitantly. "You mustn't attack. You must disregard your orders; they were improperly given."

"They were issued through command signalry of the podium. We must accept. We are programmed; we respond." The cranial turret rotated to face front again, indicating that the subject bore no further discussion.

Bollux went on doggedly. "Xim is dead! These orders of yours are wrong; they do not come from him; you cannot obey them!"

The turret swung to him again, the optical pickups betraying no emotion. "Steel-brother, we are the war-robots of Xim. No alternative is thinkable."

"Humans are not infallible. If you follow these orders, they'll lead to your destruction. Save yourselves!" He could not admit that it would be by his own hand.

The vocoder boomed. "Whether that is true or not, we carry out our orders. We are the war-robots of Xim."

The Corps Commander faced front again. "The waiting time has elapsed. Stand aside; no further delay will be tolerated." He emitted a squeal of signalry. The ranks of war-robots stepped off as one, arms swinging.

Bollux had to spring aside to keep from being trampled beneath them. His chest plastron swung open as he watched them go. "What do we do now?" Blue Max wanted to know. "Captain Solo and the others will be down there, too."

There was a quiver of sorrow in Bollux's voice modulation. "The war-robots have their built-in programming. And we, my friend, have ours."

☐ XIV

THEY had worked their way to a ridge overlooking the outer perimeter of the mining camp before Han discovered Bollux wasn't with them. Han, incensed, slipped around a spire of rock for a look at the camp. "I *told* that low-gear factory reject we needed him to monitor for sensors. Well, we're just going to have to be extra—"

Sirens began ululating throughout the camp. The travelers all hit the ground at once, but Han risked a peek around the spire. Now that they had been detected, information was more important than concealment.

The mining camp was swarming like an insect nest. Humans and other beings were running every which way to take up emergency stations. Those employees trusted by J'uoch were being issued arms and taking up defensive positions. Contract laborers were ordered by their overseers to retire across the bridge to the isolation and effective confinement of the plateau barracks area.

Han couldn't spot the sensor net he had tripped, but it was apparent that it had him pinpointed. Several reinforced fire teams were dashing to bunkers fronting Han's hiding place. Han saw that grounded near the *Millennium Falcon* and the gigantic mining lighter was another vessel, a small starship with the sleek lines of a scout.

Suddenly a response squad started up the hill to engage them, two human males with disruptor rifles, a horn-plated *W'iiri* scuttling on its six legs and bearing a grenade thrower, and an oily-skinned *Drall,* its red hide gleaming, lugging a gas projector.

Half-kneeling, half-crouching by the spire, Han dragged the old Kell Mark II around by its balance-point carrying handle. Knowing of the outdated weapon's powerful recoil, he braced himself before thumbing the firing stud. Blue energy sprang from the Kell's muzzle, tracing a broad line across the rock wall below. He was nearly knocked over backward by the Mark II's kick, but Chewbacca braced him. The rock sizzled, smoked, and shot sparks, then cracked, fragments and shards falling downslope. The response squad sought cover with gratifying freneticism.

"That should keep them off our necks until we can talk," Han judged. Cupping hand to mouth, he called out, "J'uoch! It's Solo! We have to talk, right away!"

The woman's voice, amplified by a loudhailer, rose from one of the bunkers. "Give me that log-recorder disk and throw down your guns, Solo; those are the only terms you'll get from me!"

"But she saw that we didn't have the disk," Badure muttered. "Didn't she guess that we couldn't get it from the lockbox?"

Han shouted down, "We've got no time to debate this, J'uoch; you and your whole camp are about to come under attack!" He pulled back suddenly as a barrage of small-arms fire opened up. Huddling back from it, the travelers clutched their heads in protection while energy- and projectile-searching fire probed the hillside. Rocks bubbled and exploded; shrapnel and splinters flew while explosive concussion battered their ears.

"I don't think she's going to be reasonable about this," predicted Badure.

"She's got to be," Han snapped, thinking of what would happen to his starship if the robots overran the camp.

The firing slowed for a moment, then, at some command they didn't hear, resumed even more heavily. "Face it, Solo," Hasti called to him over the din, "they want our hides and nothing less. The only way we'll get to the *Falcon* is if we can get to her while the robots are hitting the camp."

"When they're mixing it up with J'uoch's people?

We wouldn't get two meters." At that moment the firing stopped again and a voice called his name from
below.

Hasti was gazing at him in alarm. "Solo, what's
wrong? You just went pale as perma-frost."

He paid her no attention but saw by Chewbacca's
expression that the Wookiee, too, recognized the voice
of Gallandro the gunman.

"Solo! Come down and negotiate like a reasonable
fellow. We have a great deal to discuss, you and I."
The voice was calm, amused.

Han realized that sweat was beginning to bead his
brow despite the cold. A sudden suspicion hit him, and
he threw himself up into the clear for an instant, just
enough to ease the Mark II's barrel over the crest.
The response squad was on the move and another was
rushing to link up with it.

Han thumbed the trigger and hosed the barrel back
and forth randomly. The heavy-assault rifle was a
product of Dra III, made for the heavier, stronger
inhabitants of that world, with its Standard-plus gravity. The Mark II's recoil forced him back a second
time, but not before the play of its extremely powerful
beam drove the advancing squads to cover once more.

"Spread out along the ridge or they'll outflank us!"
Han ordered. His companions hurried to comply as
Gallandro's voice came again.

"I knew you wouldn't have died in something as
foolish as that uneven ship-to-ship action back at the
city, Solo. And I knew the Millennium Falcon would
draw you here in time, no matter what."

"You know just about everything, don't you?" Han
riposted.

"Except where that log-recorder is. Come, Solo; I've
struck a bargain with the delightful J'uoch here. Do
the same, don't make things difficult. And don't make
me come up there after you."

"C'mon, what's stopping you, Gallandro? There'll be
nothing left of you but those little mustache beads!"
Chewbacca and the others had taken up sniping at the
response squads, pinning them down for now, but Han

was worried about the armed aircraft in the mining camp.

The thought had no sooner formed than, scanning the sky, he saw a quick, dangerous shape swooping down at them. "Everybody down!"

The spaceboat, twin to the one that had been destroyed in the city by the lighter, made a quick preliminary pass at the ridge, its chin pods spitting. Antipersonnel rounds threw out clouds of flechettes; Han could feel the craft's afterblast as it darted by. He raised his head to see what damage it had done.

By some fortune the first pass, being hasty, had resulted in no one's being hit. But they were badly exposed there on the ridge; the next pass might well finish them all. Han pulled the heavy-assault rifle to him with a grunt of effort, pushed himself upright, and rushed out into the open on the back side of the ridge.

At the camp below, Gallandro conferred with J'uoch. "Madame, recall your boat; I'll trouble you to remember our deal." He spoke with a hint of impatience, as close to emotion as he ever let himself come. "Solo is mine, not to be killed by air attack."

Peering out of the bunker, she dismissed the objection with a wave of her hand. "What does it matter, as long as he's eliminated? My brother's using antipersonnel rounds; the log-recorder won't be damaged."

The gunman smiled, reserving his retaliation for a more convenient moment. He touched up his mustachios with a knuckle. "Solo is well armed, my dear J'uoch. You may be surprised at his resourcefulness, as may your brother."

Han raced over the open ground, keeping one eye out for available cover. Though hindered by the weight of the Mark II, he adjusted it for maximum range and power level as he ran. He had thought about handing the weapon over to the Wookiee to let him shoot at the boat, but the *Falcon*'s first mate had little liking or affinity for energy weapons, preferring his bowcaster.

Han heard the boat begin its second pass. J'uoch's brother, R'all, dove at the exposed, fleeing man. Han threw himself into a troughlike depression in the rock, the Mark II clattering down next to him. The boat flashed past, so close that Han was in the dead area between the guns' fields of fire. Flechettes burst in long lines to either side of him. R'all flashed off, adjusting his weapons for a final pass.

Han got up, braced the Mark II's buttplate against the rock, and fired. Still the heavy-assault rifle's recoil made it jump and turn; the boat was out of range before he had come anywhere near it, and now was banking for a pass that was sure to find its target.

Han hitched himself around the stone trough and pulled the Mark II's bipod legs down. He had only one more trick left, and if that didn't work, he'd have no more worries about treasure, Gallandro, or the *Falcon*. Resettling so that his knees and the small of his back were higher than his shoulders, he wrestled the Mark II around and rested it on the incline of his legs. He set his feet against the bipod legs, holding the weapon tightly to steady it.

He squinted upward through the heavy-assault rifle's open sights. The boat came at him again. He bracketed it in the sights and waited until he heard the first concussion of R'all's fire.

Then he opened up, bracing the bucking Mark II with hands and feet, holding it fairly steady for the first time. The boat's pilot recognized his danger too late; an evasive maneuver failed and the heavy-assault rifle's full force caught the light boat, tearing a long gash in the fuselage. Control circuitry and power panels erupted and a gaping hole appeared in the cockpit canopy. The boat wallowed and shook, out of control, and disappeared in a steep dive, trailing smoke and flame. A moment later the ground shook with impact.

"R'all!" J'uoch screamed to her dead brother as she clawed her way out of the bunker. The boat had exploded on impact, scattering burning debris over a long, wide swath of ground.

Gallandro caught her arm. "R'all is gone," said the gunman with no particular sympathy. "Now, we will do this thing as we originally agreed. Your ground forces will encompass Solo's position, and we'll force him out into the open and capture him alive."

She wrenched her arm away, seething with rage. "He killed my brother! I'll get Solo if I have to blow these mountains apart!" She turned and called out to her enforcer, the hulking Egome Fass, who stolidly awaited orders. "Get the crew to the loadlifter and warm up main batteries." She was about to turn from him when an unfamiliar sound, rising over the fury of the boat's destruction, made her pause. "What's that?"

Gallandro heard it, too, as did Egome Fass and all the others in the camp. It was a steady beat, shaking the ground, the pounding of metal feet. The column of Xim's war-robots appeared at a spot farther along the mining camp's perimeter, having finished their roundabout march from their mustering place.

They came in glittering ranks, arms swinging, unstoppable. When their Corps Commander gave the signal that freed them from lockstep, they spread out across the site to begin their devastation. J'uoch stared in astonishment, not quite believing what she saw. Gallandro, fingering one of the gold beads that held his mustache, tried to remain calm. "So, Solo was telling the truth after all."

Up on the ridge, Chewbacca hooted to the exhausted Han, indicating the camp. Han wearily moved to the ridge and joined his companions in looking down on a scene of utter chaos. Their own presence had been forgotten by the response squads, fire teams, and other camp defenders.

The war-robots, faithful to their instructions, moved to obliterate everything in their path. First to feel the battle machines' power was a domed building that housed repair shops. Han saw a robot smash through the dome's personnel door while a half-dozen of his comrades set to work wrenching off the rolling doors. Pieces of lockslab gave way like soggy pulp, and a group of Xim's perfect guardians moved into the dome, demolishing work areas and heavy equipment, ripping down hoisting gear, and firing with the weapons built into their metal hands. Heatbeams and particle discharges flashed, throwing weird shadows within the dome. The building flared, pitted in a score of places. The robots' fire lanced the dome, probing the sky. More of them pressed in to tear apart everything they encountered.

It was the same elsewhere in the vast mining site. The war-robots, with their limited reasoning capacity, were taking their orders literally, devoting as much attention to devastating buildings and machinery as to attacking camp personnel. Whole companies of the war machines were moving among the abandoned mining autohoppers and landgougers, tow-motors and excavators.

The robots blasted and sprayed fire everywhere, making full use of their tremendous strength. One of them was sufficient to reduce a small vehicle to rubble in moments; for larger equipment, groups cooperated. Tracks were wrenched from crawlers, whole vehicles lifted off the ground, their axles snapped, wheels ripped off, cabs torn loose, and engines yanked out of their compartments like toys. A battalion moved toward a barge shell that contained the latest shipment of refined ore. The robots tore into it, swinging and firing, wrecking everything they encountered and hurling the pieces aside.

Meanwhile, others engaged the camp personnel in determined combat, turning the camp into a scene of unbelievable chaos. War-robots flooded through the operations site. "They're headed for the *Falcon!*" Han bellowed, then charged down the ridge. Badure's shouted warnings went unheeded. Chewbacca went racing after his partner; Badure took off, too, followed by Hasti.

Skynx was left alone, staring after them. Although going after his companions seemed a good way to insure that he would never see the chrysalis stage, he realized that he had become a part of the oddly met group and felt acutely incomplete without them. Abandoning good Ruurian prudence, he flowed off after the others.

At the bottom of the slope, Han found his way blocked by one of the robots. It was just finishing demolishing one of the bunkers, kicking the fusion-formed walls to bits and hurling the larger chunks easily. The robot turned on him, its optical lenses extending a bit as their focal point adjusted. It lifted and aimed its weapon-hand.

Han quickly brought up the heavy-assault rifle and fired point-blank, knocked back several steps by the sustained recoil. His fire blazed blue against the mirror-bright chest. The machine itself was driven back a step with an electronic outburst and was ripped open. Han moved his aim up to the spot where the cranial turret was joined to the armored body.

The head came off, flying apart, smoke and flame gushing from the decapitated body. Han shot it again for good luck and the Mark II's beam came only faintly; the weapon was virtually exhausted. But it served to topple the robot, which landed with a re-sounding clatter.

More war-robots were reaching that part of the camp. Chewbacca descended to level ground, trailing dust and tumbling pebbles, just as another machine came at Han. The Wookiee threw his bowcaster to his shoulder and aimed. But his fire bounced off the ro-bot's hard breastplate; he had forgotten his weapon was still loaded with regular rounds rather than with explosives.

Han threw aside the useless assault rifle and drew his blaster, setting it for maximum power. Chewbacca stepped back, removing the magazine from his weapon and taking one of the larger ones from his bandoleer. Han stepped in front to cover him in a stiff-armed firing stance. He squeezed off bolt after bolt, deliberately and with great concentration, into the approaching robot's cranial turret. Four blaster rounds stopped the machine just as it fired in re-sponse. Han ducked the heatbeam that split the air where he had stood. As the robot fell, the beam traced a quick arc upward.

Defenders that were sufficiently well armed were putting up stiff resistance with rocket launchers, gre-nade throwers, heavy weapons, and crew-served guns. Living beings and war machines were reeling back and forth in a storm of energy discharges, bullets, shells, and fire. Four robots lifted the reinforced roof off a boxlike hut as the men defending it fired frantically. Using a chattering quad-gun, the men's shots kicked up enormous clots of ground and blew away segments of the machines even as they attacked. More robots approached to join in; the crew, with barrels depressed, traversed their gun back and forth in a frenzy, taking a terrible toll. But even though several crew members used side arms in a desperate attempt to keep from being overrun, the roofless hut was gradually outflanked and disappeared behind a wall of gleaming enemies.

Not far away, a dozen of J'uoch's employees had formed a firing line in three ranks, concentrating on any robot that came near, and were thus far succeeding in preserving their lives. Elsewhere, isolated miners worked their way among the high rocks to exchange earnest fire with the machines, which couldn't negotiate the incline.

But many of the camp personnel were caught alone or unarmed, or were surrounded. The fighting was heaviest and fiercest there, the robots' implacability matched against the furious determination of the living beings. Humans, humanoids, and nonhumanoids dodged, evaded, ran, or fought as well as they could. War-robots simply advanced, overcoming obstacles or being destroyed, without any sense of self-preservation whatsoever.

Han saw a stocky Maltorran run up behind a robot with a heavy beamdrill cradled in its brachia and press it flush against the machine's back. The robot exploded, and the drill, exploding from the backwash, killed the Maltorran. Two mining techs, a pair of human females, had gotten to a landgouger and were making a resolute effort to break through the automaton lines, crushing many of them under the gouger's tremendous treads, maneuvering to avoid their weapons' aim. But soon the fire of many robots converged on them, finding the landgouger's engine. The gouger was blown apart with an ear-splitting explosion. Elsewhere, Han saw a robot grappling with three *W'iiri* who had swarmed onto it, tearing at it with their pincers. The machine plucked them off one by one, smashing them and tossing them aside, broken and dying; but in the next moment, the robot itself toppled over, disabled by the damage they had done it.

"We'll never get through to the *Falcon!*" Badure yelled at Han. "Let's get out of here!" More robots were approaching, and to attempt a return up the steep ridge under fire would be out of the question. The old man proposed, "We can withdraw across the bridge and take shelter in the barracks area!"

Han glanced across the crevasse. "It's a dead end; there's no other way off that plateau." He considered blowing the bridge behind them, but that would take the *Millennium Falcon*'s guns, or those of the lighter.

The latter ship was herself under attack. A ring of dozens of war-robots had formed around her, furiously firing while the huge cargo ship's engines strained to lift her off, her main batteries answering the robots' fire. Many of the robots' weapons were silent, their power exhausted, but more of the machines were gathering around the lighter every moment. Though the vessel's salvos wiped out five and ten robots at a time, sending them flying in heaps of tangled, liquefied wreckage, Xim's machines kept clustering to her, weapons-hands blazing, standing their ground. Soon hundreds were massed there.

Others turned their attention to Gallandro's scoutship, cutting swaths in her hull. The lighter rose unsteadily, her shields glowing from the concentrated fire, her heavy guns raking back and forth. Just at the moment it seemed she would reach safety, one of her aged defensive shields failed; after all, the lighter was an old industrial craft, not a combat vessel. The ship became a brilliant ball of incandescence, showering torn hull fragments and molten metal into the crevasse. The detonation knocked combatants, living and machine both, to the ground. Han was on his feet again in an instant, charging toward the *Falcon* with his blaster in his hand, determined that the same thing would not happen to his beloved ship.

So was someone else. Across the battlefield a ring of war-robots was closing in on the converted freighter, preparing to demolish her, their arms raised and weapon apertures open. Others were shoving the wreckage of Gallandro's scoutship toward the brink of the crevasse.

Another machine, far smaller than they, blocked the way to the *Millennium Falcon,* seeming fragile and vulnerable. Bollux's chest plastron was open, and Blue Max's photoreceptor gazed forth. From his vocoder tumbled the signals learned from tapes shown him by Skynx, amplified by the gear Bollux had cannibalized from the podium.

The advance stopped; the war-robots waited in confusion, unable to resolve the conflicting orders. The Corps Commander appeared, the death's-head insignia of Xim gleaming on his breastplate. He loomed over Bollux. "Stand aside; everything here is to be destroyed."

"Not this vessel," Max told him in the command signalry. "This one is to be spared."

The towering robot studied the two-in-one machines. "Those were not our orders."

Max's voice, directed through the podium's scavenged horn, was high. "Orders may be amended!"

The thick arm came up, and Bollux prepared for the end of his long existence. But instead a metal finger indicated the *Falcon,* and the command came: "Spare that vessel."

With signals of acknowledgment, the other war-robots moved on. The Corps Commander still regarded the labor droid and the computer module. "I am still not sure about you two, machines. What are you?"

"Talking doorstops, if you listen to our captain's opinion," offered Blue Max.

The Corps Commander stood stock-still in surprise. "Humor? Was that not humor? What have machines become? What kind of automata are you?"

"We are your steel-brothers," Bollux put in. The Corps Commander made no further comment, but continued on his way.

The waves of robots had thwarted Han's effort to reach his ship. One, stepping over the ruins of a crew-served gun and its slain crew, advanced toward the pilot. Han was looking elsewhere, helping Hasti fire blaster and disruptor shots at a machine approaching from the opposite direction. Han's shot scored the cranial turret; Hasti's, less practiced, sent its torso and limbs in a wild scatter. Badure was firing at still another, a long-barreled power pistol in each hand.

Chewbacca stepped into the path of the oncoming robot and triggered his bowcaster. Its staves straightened, and the explosive quarrel detonated against the robot's chest armor, holing it but not stopping it. The Wookiee held his ground, jacking the foregrip of his bowcaster and firing twice more, this time hitting the robot's head and midsection. The machine came on relentlessly. Its weapons-hands were raised, but their power had been drained in battle. Chewbacca backed a step and came up against Han, who was still firing the other way.

Then the robot toppled forward. Chewbacca, standing in its very shadow, would have leaped clear but realized that Han was unaware of his imminent danger. The Wookiee shoved the pilot aside with a sweep of his hairy arm but failed himself to avoid the tottering automaton. It struck him and pinned his right arm and leg to the ground. Skynx raced to him and began pulling ineffectually at the Wookiee.

Another robot chose that moment to step over the one Han and Hasti had just downed. Since Hasti's disruptor was drained, Han moved forward, then realized that his blaster's cautionary pulser was tingling his palm in silent warning that his weapon, too, was spent.

He whirled and called to his sidekick, then saw the Wookiee wriggling to extricate himself from under the fallen robot. Chewbacca paused long enough to loft his bowcaster into the air one-handed.

Han caught it, pivoted, dropped to one knee, and pressed the stock to his cheek. He squeezed, and the explosive blast blew up against the juncture of the approaching machine's shoulder and arm. The metal limb fell away, and the robot shuddered but kept coming.

Han tried to jack the bowcaster's foregrip and

found, as had the man in the city, that his human strength was insufficient. He stopped himself from dodging out of the way; Chewbacca lay trapped, directly behind him. Badure, some distance away, couldn't hear Han's shouts for aid. Hasti fired at the machine with the only weapon she had left, the dart-shooter, but emptying the whole clip at it served no purpose.

Han avoided Chewbacca's efforts to swipe him out of the way and shifted his grip on the bowcaster, preparing for a last, hopeless defense.

☐ XV

THE war-robot seemed to block out the sky, a machine out of nightmare. But abruptly its cranial turret flew apart in a blast of charred circuitry and ruptured power routing as a thread-thin, precisely aimed beam found its most vulnerable point. Han scarcely had the presence of mind to take a step back, nearly treading on Chewbacca, as the automaton crashed at his feet like an old tree.

He leaped up onto its back and scanned the battlefield. Far across it, a form in gray waved once.

"Gallandro!" The gunman gave him a bare, stark smile that held nothing Han could read. Han drew without thinking, then remembered his blaster was empty. Just then a robot appeared behind Gallandro, closing in on him, arms wide. Han never made a conscious decision, but pointed and shouted a warning.

The gunman was too far away to have heard, but he saw Han's expression and understood. He spun and ducked instinctively. The robot just missed with a blow of enormous power. With an incredible display of agility and reflexes, Gallandro seized the arm and rode the robot's recovery-backswing, at the same time putting two quick shots into its head. Letting go, he was flung clear to land lightly and put a last bolt into the robot as it fell.

Han watched the incident with awe. By far the most dangerous machine there was Gallandro. The gunman gave Han a sardonic bow and a mocking grin, then, like a ghost, was gone again in the swirl of battle.

The air was hot with the unleashed energies of the battle. With Skynx's and Badure's help, Chewbacca had squirmed free of the fallen robot, while Hasti stood nervous guard. Taking back his bowcaster, the Wookiee made a quick motion toward the robot that had so narrowly missed nailing Han and barked a question.

"It was *him*, Gallandro," Han told his partner. "A fifty-, maybe sixty-meter tight-beam shot." The Wookiee shook his head in bewilderment, mane flying.

There was nowhere to go except the camp living area, across the bridge. "Will you two stop chatting and get going?" Hasti called. "They'll have us surrounded if we don't hurry."

They started for the bridge at the best pace they could manage, a half-trot, each of them bearing a number of minor injuries and wounds. They moved in a defensive ring, Badure at the leading edge with his power pistols, Hasti to his right and Skynx to his left, with Chewbacca and Han bringing up the rear, back-pedaling and sideskipping. A metallic voice called Han's name.

Bollux somehow injected a note of immense relief into his vocoder drawl. "We're so glad you're all safe. The *Millennium Falcon*'s unharmed, at least for the time being, but I don't know how long that will last. Unfortunately, it's inaccessible just now."

Han wanted to know exactly what that meant, but Bollux interrupted. "No time for that now. I have the means to remedy our situation, sir," he told the pilot, resettling the signalry equipment he had taken from the robots' command podium. "But you'll have to get to the far side of the bridge before I can use it."

"You're on, Bollux! All right, everybody, scratch gravel!" They hastened away. The attack hadn't gotten as far as the bridge yet, but resistance was crumbling rapidly.

At the bridgehead Bollux paused. "I'll be staying here, sir. The rest of you must proceed across."

Han looked around. "What're you going to do, talk them into suicide? You better stay with us; we'll take to the high ground on the plateau."

With a strange sincerity, the droid refused. "Thank you for your concern, sir; Max and I are flattered. But we have no intention of being destroyed, I assure you."

Han felt ridiculous for arguing with a droid, but insisted, "This is no place to get noble, old-timer."

Seeing the war-robots converging on them, Bollux persevered. "I really must insist that you go, sir; our basic programming won't permit Max and me to see you come to harm here."

They departed unwillingly. Hasti walked with the tired Skynx beside her. Badure patted the droid's hard shoulder and trudged off, and Chewbacca waved a paw. "Look after Max," Han said, "and don't get yourself junked, old fellow."

Bollux watched them go, then searched among the rocks and boulders for a place of concealment at that end of the bridge.

Han and his companions slogged wearily across the bridge among others who had survived the robots' onslaught and were now falling back for a final stand. At the halfway point they came upon the body of a fallen mining tech who had died before she could complete the crossing, a *T'rinn* whose bright plumage was now charred and burned from combat. Han gently took a shoulder-fired rocket launcher from her lifeless claws, the weapon still containing a half-magazine of rockets. He was just standing up when a figure broke from the stream of retreating miners and attacked him, swinging an empty needlebeamer.

"Murderer!" J'uoch shrieked, her first blow grazing the pilot over the ear before he was aware of her onset. "You killed my brother! I'll kill you, you filthy animal!" Dazed, he pushed himself backward to avoid the blows she was raining on him, forearm up to protect himself.

Chewbacca would have torn the hysterical woman from his friend, but at the same moment he was struck from behind, a heavy blow from a thick forearm. The Wookiee fell to his knees, losing his bowcaster, as a huge weight fell upon him: Egome Fass, the enforcer. The two huge creatures rolled over and over, wrestling, tearing at one another. Retreating miners skirted the struggles, concerned only with staying alive.

Badure, weakened by the ordeal, waved an unsteady power pistol at J'uoch. But before he could fire, Hasti had thrown herself at the woman who had killed her sister Lanni. They whirled and fought, hacking and kicking at each other, finding reserves of strength in their mutual hatred.

Badure pulled Han up just as J'uoch got her forearm around Hasti's throat. But Hasti writhed free of the hold, dropped and turned, put her head and shoulder against the other's midsection and drove her back with feet churning and driving. J'uoch was shoved backward against the bridge's waist-high railing and toppled over it. She fell screaming, in a flurry of coveralls, reaching and thrashing. Hasti's momentum had carried her halfway over the rail, too.

Badure was there in time to pull her back from the rail, grabbing the material of her clothes. She sobbed for breath, her pulse pounding. Then it came to her that the roaring she heard wasn't in her ears. Chewbacca and Egome Fass had gone to war.

It had been the second time J'uoch's enforcer had struck the Wookiee from behind. What the *Falcon*'s first mate felt now could only pallidly be described as outrage. Han waved Badure off when the old man would have shot Egome Fass.

The two punched and grasped at one another while Han leaned against the rail to watch the honor match. "Aren't you going to help him?" Hasti puffed, her face showing the scratches and abrasions of her own match.

"Chewie wouldn't appreciate that," Han told her, keeping one eye on the rallying of robots at the end of the bridge. But he eased a pistol from Badure's belt in case the match didn't go as it should.

Egome Fass had gotten a choke-hold on Chewbacca. Rather than squirm out of it or apply an infighting trick, the Wookiee chose to lock both hands on his opponent's arm and turn it into a contest of pure strength. Egome Fass was bulkier, Chewbacca more agile, but the question of brute force was still open. Their arms quivered and muscles jumped in the straining backs.

Bit by bit the arm was levered away from Chewbacca's throat. The Wookiee showed his fangs in savage triumph, and burst free of the hold. But Egome Fass wasn't done with tests of strength. He lunged at his antagonist for a deadly hug. Chewbacca accepted it.

They staggered back and forth, first the Wookiee's feet leaving the bridge, then the enforcer's. Both applied their full brawn in fearsome constriction. Egome Fass's feet were lifted clear of the bridge and stayed that way as the Wookiee held him aloft, muscles standing out like cables under Chewbacca's pelt. The enforcer's struggle became more frantic, less aggressive. Panic crept into his movements. Then there was a crack, and Egome Fass's body slumped. Chewbacca let go, and the enforcer slid limply to the bridge's surface. The Wookiee had to rest a paw on a support to steady himself.

Han teetered over with the rocket launcher over one shoulder. "You're getting decrepit; two tries to put away a bum like that!" He laughed and affectionately punched the Wookiee's shoulder.

"Enough, enough!" Skynx protested, tugging at Han's red-seamed trouser leg. "The robots are ready to attack; Bollux said we must be across the bridge."

Han didn't know how much chance the labor droid stood of stopping the steel horde, but he and the others obeyed Skynx's pleas. There was no one to stand with them at the end of the bridge. The miners who had reached it had gone either to put up barricades in the buildings or to find safe places among the rocks.

Han stopped as soon as his boots were off the bridge. He sat on the ground, looking back across the bridge. "We might as well face it here."

No one made any objection. Badure gave Hasti one of his pistols, while Chewbacca fitted a new magazine into his bowcaster. Hasti put one arm around Han's neck and kissed his cheek. "That's for a good try," she explained.

Bollux crouched in the jumble of boulders on the far side of the bridge. The mining-operations site was now completely razed. Machinery was burned and buildings were flattened, and no living thing could be seen.

The Corps Commander had mustered all his forces with high-pitched summonses. Other resistance had been crushed; all that remained was to annihilate the barracks area on the far side of the bridge, the successful completion of their first combat action in generations.

Bollux waited and didn't try to interfere. That would have been useless, he knew; they weren't so different from him. The machines gathered around their commander by the hundreds. The Corps Commander indicated the way with a long metal arm, gleaming like a statue of death in the blue-white light. He stumped toward the bridge, and his awesome troops crowded after him. And as the war-robots drew abreast of him, about to step onto the bridge, Bollux triggered the command signalry he had brought from the podium.

The Corps Commander fell into a marching step as the signals reached him. He didn't question them; the commands were automatic, military, geared to a segment of him that didn't doubt or ponder. Such was his construction.

Behind their commander the other war-robots responded to the signal as well, falling into ranks of ten, in step with their leader. Funneled onto the bridge, their ranks filled it from side to side. They stepped with meticulous precision. Metal feet tramped; arms swung in time.

"Will it work?" Bollux asked his friend.

Blue Max, tuned in with both their audio pickups, listened carefully, cautioning the droid not to bother him at this critical point. At Max's instruction, Bollux adjusted the marching tempo, matching the forced vibration of the robots' tread to the bridge's own natural frequency, creating a powerful resonance. The war-robots marched on to do battle for an overlord generations dead. The bridge began to quake, dust rising and forming a haze with the unified footfalls. Timbers reverberated, joints and stress members strained; the perfection of their marching made the robots a single, unimaginable power hammer. More of them poured onto the bridge and took up the step, adding to the concussions.

At last the bridge itself thrummed under them as Max found the perfect beat. All the robots were on the bridge, with no thought but to get to the other side and attack the enemy.

Han and the others rose, waiting. "I guess Bollux couldn't pull off his plan," Han said. The front rank, following their gleaming leader, had grown large. "We'll have to fall back."

"There's not much room for that," Hasti reminded him sadly. He had no answer.

Suddenly Skynx exclaimed. "Look!"

Han did, feeling a deep vibration through his boots. The bridge was shuddering in time with the robots' march, its timbers creaking and cracking with the punishment it couldn't absorb. Feet pounding, the robots marched on.

Then there was a rending snap; the vibration had found a member that couldn't support it. A timber bent and turned in its bed of press-poured material. The bed wouldn't accept the play and the timber twisted and split. All the supporting members at that side of the bridge gave way.

There were electronic bleats of distress from the war machines and the popping of aged rivets from the timber-joining plates. For a moment the whole doomed assemblage, robots and bridge, was suspended in space. Then all fell into the crevasse with a huge concussion, sending up clouds of rock dust and smoke and a wall of impact-noise that drove Han back from the crevasse's edge.

Wiping the dust from his eyes and spitting it out of his mouth, Han returned to the brink. Among the drifted dust and smoke he could see bridge timbers and the gleam of crumpled armor, the flare of circuit fires, overloaded power packs, broken leads, and shorted weapons. Suddenly Bollux appeared at the other side of the crevasse, waving stiffly, having divested himself of the scavenged equipment. Han returned the wave, laughing. *From now on those two are full crewmembers.*

A new sound made him look around in surprise and anger, mouthing a Corellian oath. The *Millennium Falcon* was lifting off. She rose on blaring thrusters, swinging out over the abyss. Han and Chewbacca watched in despair as they saw their ship whisked from under their noses despite all their efforts.

But the freighter settled gently on their side of the crevasse. They got to her just as her ramp-bay doors opened and the main ramp lowered, beneath and astern the cockpit. The main hatch rolled up, and there stood Gallandro. He welcomed them with a smile, his weapon conspicuously holstered. His fine clothing and beautiful scarf were soiled, but other than that, Han reflected, he looked none the worse for someone who had just waded through a horde of war-robots.

The gunman sketched a mocking bow. "I found myself obliged to play dead among the slain; I couldn't get to the ship until the robots had all left, or I'd have been of more assistance. Solo, those droids of yours are priceless!" His smile disappeared. "And so is Xim's treasure, eh? You're out for high stakes for a change; my compliments."

"You tracked me all the way from the Corporate Sector to tell me that?" Chewbacca had his bowcaster aimed at Gallandro, but Han knew that even that was no guarantee against the man's incredible speedraw.

The gunman made a wry twist of his mouth. "Not originally. I was rather upset about our encounter there. But I'm a man of reason; I'm prepared to put that aside in view of the amount of money involved. Bring me in for a full cut and we forget the grudge. And you get your ship back; wouldn't that strike you as a fair arrangement?"

Han remained suspicious. "All of a sudden you're ready to kiss and make up?"

"The treasure, Solo, the treasure. The wealth of Xim would buy affection from anyone. All other considerations are secondary; surely that's in keeping with your own philosophy, isn't it?"

Han was confused. Hasti, who had come up behind him, said, "Don't trust him!"

Gallandro turned clear blue eyes on her. "Ah, the young lady! If he doesn't accept my offer, you'll be in a bad way as well, my dear; this vessel's weapons are functional." His voice went cold, the playacting evaporating. "Decide," he ordered Han crisply.

The defenders were beginning to emerge from the barracks, having seen the bridge collapse and the ship land. In another moment, escape might be much more complicated. Han reached out and pushed down Chewbacca's bowcaster. "Everybody onboard; we're back in business."

In moments they had lifted off with Han at the controls, uttering angry maledictions at the techs who had torn the starship apart in search of the log-recorder disk and reassembled her so inexpertly. "Why did J'uoch have the ship repaired, anyway?" Badure asked.

"She was either going to keep it for her own use or sell it," explained Gallandro. "She tried to sell me a lame story about her disagreements with you people, but considering the things I'd already discovered about your movements, the truth wasn't hard to guess."

Han brought the ship in to hover over the camp. "What about the other miners, the ones who lived?" Hasti asked.

"They've got food, weapons, supplies there," Badure said. "They can hold out until a ship shows up, or slog it over to the city."

Han was bringing the *Falcon* down again on the other side of the crevasse. A gleaming metal form waited there. Chewbacca went aft to let Bollux aboard.

"Like you said," Han found himself telling Gallandro defensively, "they're valuable droids."

"I said 'priceless,'" Gallandro corrected him. "Now that we're comrades, I'd never offend you by suggesting you've gone soft. May I inquire what our next move is?"

"Direct collection of intelligence data," Han declared, lifting off again. "Interrogation of indigenous personnel for tactical information. We're going to make a couple of locals sweat and find out what all this was about."

The Survivors who had activated the war-robots had decided to escape together in one large hover-raft rather than spread out across the plains in a fleet. A few passes and a barrage from the *Falcon*'s belly turret brought them to a halt. They threw down their arms and waited.

Han prudently left Chewbacca at the ship's controls. He and the others, weapons recharged, went to confront the Survivors. Hasti, first down the ramp, waved her gun at them, shouting, and fairly dragged one of them off the raft. Han and Badure had to pull her off the man, while Gallandro looked on in amusement and Skynx in confusion.

"It's him, I tell you," she yelled, straining to go after the frightened man again. "I recognize the white blaze in his hair. It's the vault steward's assistant."

"Well, clubbing him silly isn't going to help," Han pointed out as he turned to the man. "Better spill it, or I'll let her loose."

The assistant licked dry lips. "I can say nothing, I swear! We are conditioned in youth not to reveal the secrets of the Survivors."

"Old-fashioned hypno," Han dismissed it, "nothing you can't overcome if we scare you enough."

Gallandro stepped forward with a wintry smile, pulling his pistol in one fluid motion, adjusting it one-handed. A low-power, high-resolution beam sizzled into the ground at the captive's feet, blackening and curling the grass. The man paled.

Bollux had come up, his chest plastron open. "There's a better way," Blue Max advised. "Circumvent his conditioning, and we can find out anything we want. We can rig up a strobe and key it to the same light pattern the Survivors use."

Gallandro was dubious. "Query, computer: can you duplicate the Survivors' light pulses exactly?"

"Quit talking to me like I'm some kind of *appliance!*" snarled Max.

"Beg pardon," said Gallandro politely. "I keep forgetting. Shall we proceed?"

☐ XVI

THE *Millennium Falcon* moved through the Dellaltian air at what was for her a conservative speed. Even so, Han was recovering the distance from the city in minutes.

Gallandro was off gathering equipment elsewhere in the ship, with Bollux's help. Hasti and Badure sat, respectively, in the navigator's and communication officers' high-backed chairs behind Han and Chewbacca. Skynx, his injuries dressed and treated, as theirs had been, was curled in Hasti's lap.

"It's hard to accept," Hasti was saying. "All these years. How could a secret be kept for generations?"

"Secrets have been kept for ages," Badure pointed out. "It was easy enough in this case; there're really two strata in the Survivors' organization. The dupes lived and died there in the mountains, maintaining the war-robots as a religious ritual, holding their ceremonies once in a while. Then there were the others, the ones who knew the secret of Xim's treasure and waited for the time they could use it."

"But they all got the conditioning as children, right?" Han asked.

"And when Lanni happened on the mountain base and got her hands on the log-recorder disk and put it in the lockbox at the vaults," Hasti murmured, her voice thick with sorrow, "she couldn't have known that the steward was part of the Survivors' apparatus."

Such had been the assistant's testimony once his conditioning had been overcome. The steward had sent the disk back to the Survivors' mountain warren as soon as it had come into his possession, of course. And he had contrived a nonexistent voice-coder to keep

Lanni, Hasti, or anyone else from claiming it. He was aware that J'uoch had learned something about the disk from Lanni before killing her, and that the woman was actively seeking it. He had passed word to her through Survivor double agents that the *Millennium Falcon* had landed, knowing he couldn't cope with the starship if force were brought to bear on the vaults. He knew J'uoch could, and hoped that Hasti and the others and their ship would be destroyed in battle, and the matter closed.

But instead, J'uoch had mounted the ambush that had resulted in the capture of the *Falcon*. Not having found the disk onboard the starship, J'uoch had made pointed inquiries at the vaults. The steward had managed to put her off but, knowing it was only a matter of time until she used force to inspect the lockboxes herself and put him to a more harrowing interrogation, he ordered the long-dormant Guardian Corps sent out against the mining camp. The war-robots, maintained through generations for just such an emergency, had come close to accomplishing their purpose.

"So why are the Survivors still sitting on their money after all this time?" Han wondered.

"The Old Republic was stable and unbeatable," Badure answered. "They had no hope of moving against it, even with Xim's treasure backing them. It's only now, with the Empire having its troubles, that the Survivors smelled a setup they might be able to exploit, especially here in the Tion Hegemony. I bet small-timers everywhere are getting the same sort of idea."

"A new Xim, and a new despotism," Hasti mused. "How could they have believed it, even under conditioning?"

"They can believe one thing," Han said, watching the land roll by quickly beneath them. "The Survivors are about to suffer a capital loss."

"Shouldn't we have a bigger ship?" Hasti inquired.

Han shook his head. "First we make sure the treasure's there, and put what we can in the *Falcon*. Then we unship a quad-battery and some defensive shielding generators. Gallandro and I will hold the fort while Chewie and the rest of you go find a bigger ship, about the size of J'uoch's lighter, say. It won't take too long."

"And what will you do with your share of the money?" Badure asked casually. He saw doubt and confusion cross the pilot's face.

"I'll worry about that when I've got a stack of credits so high I'll have to rent a warehouse," Han replied at last.

Gallandro, who had just entered the cockpit, carrying the equipment he had gathered, said, "Well put, Solo! Indelicate, but on target." He checked their progress. "We'll be there in a moment. I haven't ransacked a bank in a long time; there's a certain zest to it."

Han reserved his reply and put the starship into a steep dive. The *Falcon* dropped out of the sky ahead of her own sonic boom. Dellaltians near the vaults suddenly saw the vessel appear above them, its braking thrusters thundering, its landing gear extended like predatory claws. People scurried for shelter as the shock wave of the freighter's passage caught up with her, making the ground tremble and the buildings shake. She came to rest on the roofless portico outside the vaults' single door.

The *Falcon*'s external speakers whooped and wailed with emergency sirens and klaxons. Her visual warning systems and running lights were flashing at maximum luminescence. Bystanders would have difficulty seeing and hearing, much less interfering.

The ramp dropped and Han and Gallandro ran down, blasters ready, equipment and tools weighting them. Behind followed Badure, Hasti, and Skynx. The girl objected, "Are you sure there isn't some other way to do this?" Han had to read her lips, unable to hear her in the din.

He shook his head. Chewbacca had to stay at the controls, both because he knew the ship and because Han trusted only the Wookiee with care of the *Falcon*. Bollux stayed behind as well to keep a photoreceptor on instrumentation the first mate couldn't spare time to monitor. Han wanted at least two people to hold the main door, Hasti and Badure. He and Gallandro would do the searching, taking Skynx along to translate.

The area seemed fairly secure; the Dellaltians had no way to cope with an armed starship. Han waved to his partner in the cockpit, and though he couldn't be heard, added, "Fire, Chewie!"

From the *Falcon*'s top and belly turrets shot lines of red annihilation, playing on the closed door of the treasure vault. Smoke obscured the door in seconds as the quad-guns traced incandescent lines across it. Red cannonfire pitted and burned through material that had withstood generations of time and weathering, cutting glowing gashes in it. No weapon of its time could have penetrated it so easily, but in moments the door had been breached, pieces of it falling away. The reports of the gunfire added to the tremendous noise level.

Han signaled again and Chewbacca ceased fire. Smoke billowed away on the chill wind to reveal a yawning hole, its red-hot edges quickly cooling. "Armed robbery!" laughed Gallandro. "There's nothing like it!"

"Let's get inside," Han mouthed. They ran together and hurdled through the gaping door. Hasti and Badure followed a moment later. "Stay here and make sure you maintain comlink with Chewie," Han told them. Badure set Skynx down.

"Don't forget the defensive system!" Hasti called as Han, Gallandro, and Skynx raced off. Among the things their captives had revealed was the fact that the treasure vaults were equipped with defensive security devices; the presence of a firearm in any protected area would trigger automated weapons.

They went deeper into the gloom of the cavernous vestibule, abandoned by the Dellaltians, who had wisely sought other refuge. Han didn't see a man appear to one side, weapon raised, but Gallandro caught the movement, drew, and fired all in the same instant. The steward cried aloud, clutching his middle, then

collapsing to the pressure-pacted tile floor. The gunman kicked the steward's dropped disruptor away.

"You cannot, cannot," the white-bearded man
moaned, half in delirium from his wound. "We have
kept it, safe, unsullied since we were entrusted with it."
His lids fluttered and lowered forever.

Gallandro laughed. "We'll make better use of it than
you, old man. At least we'll get it into circulation, eh,
Solo?"

Han, moving on, offered no answer. Gallandro came
after, and Skynx rushed to catch up. They descended
dusty ramps and broad staircases, the empty vaults all
around them. At one point they lowered themselves by
the cable of an ancient lift platform that no longer
worked, complying precisely with the instructions ex-
tracted from the captive Survivors under hypno. Han
marked their trail with a tint bulb. At the lowest level
of the vault proper they came to a forking of the ways.
Their information on the vault-complex layout went no
further than this.

"It's off this corridor, one of the side tunnels," Han
said. "Got your copy of the identi-marks? Good."

"The little fellow can stay with you, Solo," Gallandro replied, meaning Skynx. "I prefer to operate
alone." He hitched up the straps holding his equipment and stalked away.

"Okay, stay sharp," Han told Skynx, and the search
began. Soon they were absorbed in the intricate business of examining side corridors for the identi-marks
described by their prisoners and copied by Skynx.
These lowest levels of the vault proper were stale and
seemed airless, layered with ankle-deep dust, and a
gloom that resisted the beam of the hand-held spot-
light. They passed room after room of empty bins and
vacant shelves.

At last Skynx stopped. "Captain, this is it! These
are the ones!" He was vibrating with excitement. To
Han the side corridor looked no different than any
other, ending as it did in a blank wall at the bottom of
an obviously empty vault complex. But Skynx was
right; the identi-marks matched. Han shucked his
other gear and lifted a heavy-duty fusion cutter into

place. Skynx, taking the comlink, tried to contact the others and inform them of the find, but could raise no response.

"The walls are probably too thick," Han suggested as he set to work. When it had been built, the wall would have withstood any assault that could have been made with portable equipment, but Han was beneficiary of a long technological gap. Chunks of the wall began to fall away. Beyond was the glow of a perpetual illumi-system.

Han set the fusion cutter aside hurriedly, anxious to see for himself. A treasure beyond spending! He could barely contain himself. He ducked and stepped through, followed by Skynx. The vault was dust-free, dry, and as quiet as when Xim's artisans had sealed it, moments before they were put to death, centuries ago.

His steps echoing in the stillness, Han smiled. "The *real* vaults; all the time they were right here!" Hunters had scoured this whole part of space for Xim's treasure because his vaults were empty and all the time there had been complete duplicates, right under the decoys. "Skynx, I'll buy you a planet to play with!"

The Ruurian made no answer, silenced by the weight of years hanging over the place. They followed the corridor through a few turns and came to a stretch where warning flashers blinked in their wall sockets, as they had been doing for centuries. This no-weapons zone was an antechamber to the true treasure vaults of Xim.

Han stopped, wishing neither to be burned by the defensive weapons nor to go on unarmed, aware he might face other dangers. He turned back with great reluctance. At the fusion-cut opening, Gallandro waited.

Han paused and Skynx waited uncertainly. "We found it," the pilot told the gunman with a jerk of his thumb. "The real one. It's back there." He realized Gallandro had heard Skynx's transmissions after all.

Gallandro registered no elation, only amused acceptance. Han knew without being told that everything had changed. The gunman's abandoned equipment was stacked to one side, and he had doffed his short jacket, prelude to a gun duel. "I said, the *treasure* is back there," Han repeated.

Gallandro smiled his frosty smile. "This has nothing to do with money, Solo, although I postponed it until you and your group could help me find the vaults. I have my own plans for Xim's treasure."

Han warily shrugged out of his jacket. "Why?" was all he asked, carefully unsnapping his holster's retaining strap and rotating it forward out of his way. His fingers stretched and worked, waiting.

"You require chastening, Solo. *Who do you think you are?* Truth to tell, you're nothing but a commonplace outlaw. Your luck has run out: now, call the play!"

Han nodded, knowing Gallandro would if he didn't. "And this'll make you feel superior, right?" His hand blurred for his blaster, the best single play of his life.

Their speedraw mechanics were very different. Han's incorporated movements of shoulders and knees, a slight dipping, a partial twist. Gallandro's was ruthless economy, an explosion of every nerve and muscle that moved his right arm alone.

When the blaster bolt slammed into his shoulder, Han's overwhelming reaction was surprise; some part of him had believed in his luck to the end. His own draw half-completed, his shot went into the floor. He was spun half around, in shock, smelling the stench of his own charred flesh. The pain of the wound started an instant later. A second bolt from the cautious Gallandro struck his forearm and Han's blaster dropped.

Han sank to his knees, too startled to cry out. Skynx retreated with a terrified chitter. Swaying, clasping his wounded arm to him, Han heard Gallandro say, "That was very good, Solo; you came closer than anyone's come in a long time. But now I'll take you back to the Corporate Sector—not that I care about the Authority's justice, but there are those who have to be shown what it means to stand in my way."

Han gasped through locked teeth, "I'm not doing time in any Authority horror factory."

Gallandro ignored that. "Your friends are more

expendable, however. If you'll pardon me, I'll have to see to your Ruurian comrade before he gets into any mischief."

He slapped a pair of binders he'd found onboard the *Falcon* around Han's ankles and ground the pilot's comlink under his heel. "You were never the amoralist you feigned to be, Solo, but I am. In a way, it's too bad we didn't meet later, when you were salted and wiser. You're pretty good in a fight; you might've made a useful lieutenant." He removed the charge from Han's blaster, tucked it into his belt, and sauntered off after Skynx, who, unable to get past the gunman, had fled back down the corridors toward the treasure vaults.

Gallandro moved cautiously, knowing the Ruurian was unarmed but counting no being harmless when it was fighting for its life. He rounded a corner to see Skynx cowering against the wall some distance along, gazing at him with huge, terrified eyes, paralyzed with fear. Around the far turn of the corridor he could see the reflected warning lights of a no-weapons zone.

Gripping his blaster, Gallandro smirked. "It's a pity, my little friend, but there's too much at stake here: Solo's the only one I can afford to take alive. I shall make this as easy as I can. Hold still."

Drawing a bead on Skynx's head, he stepped forward. Energy discharges flashed from hidden emplacements; even Gallandro's fabulous reflexes gave him no edge against the speed of light.

Caught in a flaring crossfire of defensive weapons, the gunman was hit by a dozen lethal blasts before he could so much as move. He was the center of an abrupt inferno, then his scorched remains fell to the corridor floor and the smell of incinerated flesh clogged the air.

Skynx uncoiled from his spot at the corridor wall bit by bit. He threw aside the warning flashers he had removed from their sockets along the corridor's wall. He gave silent thanks Gallandro hadn't noticed the empty sockets; a prudent Ruurian probably would have.

"Humans," remarked Skynx, then went off to rescue Han Solo.

"Not much left of him, is there?" Han asked rhetorically an hour later as he stood over Gallandro's blackened remains. Like the others, he had left his gun outside the no-weapons zone. Badure and Hasti had made temporary repairs to his shoulder and forearm with one of the ship's medi-packs. If Han received competent medical attention soon, there would be no lasting effect from Gallandro's blaster bolts.

Chewbacca was just finishing a careful examination of that corridor and the one beyond, running a thorough check along the walls to search out each weapons emplacement. He had opened each one with hand tools and deactivated it. Satisfied that there would be no danger in bringing power equipment and tools inside, the Wookiee barked to Han.

"Let's get busy; I don't like the idea of the *Falcon* being unmanned." When Skynx had returned with news of the gun duel, Chewbacca had moved the starship so that she blocked the main door, her ramp extended down through it. He had warped the ship's defensive mantle around and set her guns to fire automatically on sensor-lock should anyone come too close, one warning volley and then the real item. The Dellaltians trapped inside on the starship's arrival had already surrendered and been permitted to leave; the *Falcon* would protect the treasure hunters for the time being, but Han didn't want to press his already overextended luck.

They gathered their gear and moved on. At the end of the next corridor was a metal wall bearing a Wookiee-high representation of Xim's death's-head symbol. Chewbacca lifted the fusion cutter to it and began slicing, splitting the insignia in two amid flying, flashing motes. Then he began carving in earnest. Heat washed back across him.

In short order there was a wide opening in the door. Beyond, bathed in the glow of illumi-panels that had been keeping the place bright for generations, was the glittering of gems, the gleam of metals, piles of strong-

boxes, and racks of storage cylinders in warehouse-
sized shelf stacks that stretched from floor to high
ceiling and away into the distance as far as they could
see.

And this was only the first of the treasure rooms.

Skynx was quiet, almost reverent. He had made the
find of a lifetime, a discovery out of daydreams.
Badure and Hasti remained solemn, too, as they considered the size and wealth of the place, the impact
it would have on their lives, and the memory of what
they had gone through to stand here.

Not so Han and Chewbacca. The pilot jumped
through the gap in the door, wounded arm held to
him by a traction web. "We did it! We did it!" he
shouted in glee. The Wookiee lurched after him, tossing his long-maned head back with an ecstatic
"Rooo-oo!" They slapped each other, laughter echoing
away into the piles of treasure. Chewbacca's huge feet
slapped the floors in a thumping victory dance as Han
laughed in joy.

Skynx and Badure had gone to open containers
with Bollux's help, to examine Xim's spoils. Chewbacca offered to assist them. "Spread it out here!" Han
enjoined him. "I want to roll around in it!"

He paused when he noticed Hasti nearby, eying him
strangely. "I always wondered what you'd be like,"
she told him, "when you found your big win, you
and the Wook. What now?"

Han still rode the wave of elation. *"What now?
Why, we'll, we'll—"* He stopped, giving the subject
some serious thought for the first time. "We'll pay off
our debts, get ourselves a first-class ship and crew,
uh . . ."

Hasti nodded to herself. "And settle down, Han?"
she asked softly. "Buy a planet, or take over a few
conglomerates and live the life of a good man of business?" She shook her head slowly. "Your problems
are just beginning, rich man."

His joy was receding fast, replaced by a tangled
knot of doubts, plans, the need for forethought and
mature wisdom. But before he could berate Hasti for
being a spoilsport, he heard Chewbacca's angry roar.

The Wookiee held a metallic ingot, frowning at it in disgust. He dumped a handful of them onto the floor in a chiming avalanche and gave the pile a kick that sent ingots skittering every which way. Han forgot Hasti and went to his friend. "What is it?"

Chewbacca explained with frustrated grunts and moans. Han picked up one of the ingots and saw that his copilot was right. "This stuff's *kiirium!* You can get it anywhere; Skynx, what's it doing in with the treasure?"

The small academician had located a vault-directory screen at the end of the nearest shelf stack, an old televiewer mounted on a low stand. He brought it to flickering life, and columns of ciphers and characters raced across the screen as Skynx answered distractedly.

"There would seem to be a great deal of it here, Captain. And a huge quantity of mytag crystalline vertices and mountains of enriched bordhell-type fuel slugs, among other things."

"Mytag crystals?" Han repeated in puzzlement. "They run those things off by the carload; what kind of treasure's this? Where's the *real* treasure?"

A belly laugh distracted him. Badure had found a canister of the mytag crystal and flung a double handful into the air. The crystals rained down around him, catching the light, as he convulsed in laughter. "This *is* it! Or was, an age ago. Don't you see, Slick? Kiirium is artificial shielding material, not very good by modern standards but a major breakthrough in its time, and tough to produce to boot. With quantities of kiirium to shield heavy guns and engines, Xim could field warcraft that were better armed and faster than anything else in space at the time.

"And mytag crystals were used in old subspace commo and detection gear; you needed lots and lots of them for any spacefleet or planetary defenses. And so forth; all this was critical war materiél. With the stuff in these vaults, Xim could have assembled a war machine that would have conquered this whole part of space. But he lost big at the Third Battle of Vontor, first."

"That's *it?*" Han bellowed. "We went through all this for a treasure that's *obsolete?*"

"Not quite," Skynx commented mildly, still bent over the screen. "One whole section is filled with information tapes, art works, and artifacts. There is a hundred times more information contained here than everything we know about that period altogether."

"I'll bet the Survivors have long since forgotten just what it was they were guarding," Hasti put in. "They believed the legends, just like everyone else. I wonder what did happen to the *Queen of Ranroon?*"

Badure shrugged. "Perhaps they plunged her into the system's primary after she offloaded the treasure, or sent her off with a skeleton crew to arrange misleading sightings of her and create a false trail. Who knows?"

Skynx had left the viewscreen and started a delirious dance, first on his hind limbs, then on the front ones, hopping and capering much as Han and Chewbacca had a moment before. "Marvelous! Miraculous! What a *find!* I'm sure to get my own chair funded—no, my own *department!*"

Han, leaning against a wall, slowly sank to a squatting position. "Artworks, hmm? Chewie and I can just stroll into the Imperial Museum with a bunch under our arms and start haggling, right?" He rested his forehead on his good arm. Chewbacca patted his shoulder solicitously, making mournful sounds.

Skynx gradually stopped cavorting, realizing what a disappointment all this was to the two. "There *are* some things of intrinsic value, Captain. If you choose carefully, you could fill your ship with items you could dispose of relatively simply. There would be some profit." He was fighting the urge to hoard the entire find, knowing that the *Millennium Falcon* could bear away no more than an insignificant part of it. "Enough, I suppose, to get your ship repaired properly and have your wounds looked after in a first-class medicenter."

"What about us?" Hasti interposed. "Badure and I haven't even got a starship."

Skynx pondered for a moment, then brightened. "I

can write my own ticket with the university, an un-
limited budget. How would you two like to work with
me? Academic pursuits will be dull after this, I suppose, to a pair of humans. But there'd be generous pay
and retirement benefits and quick promotions. We'll be
years and years working on this find. I'll need someone
to look after all the workers, scholars, and automata."
Badure smiled and put an arm around Hasti's shoulders. She nodded.

That made Skynx think of something else. "Bollux,
would you and Blue Max care for positions? You'd be
of great help, I'm sure. After all, you two are the only
ones who interacted with the war-robots at any length.
There's certain to be an effort to study their remains;
we have a great deal yet to learn about their thought
processes."

Blue Max answered for them both. "Skynx, we'd
like that a lot."

"If the locals don't march in here and take it all
away from you," Han reminded them, as Chewbacca
helped him to his feet. Seeing their concern, he added,
"I guess we'll leave you a portable defensive generator
and some heavy weapons and supplies out of the
Falcon. That'll give us more cargo space."

Badure sounded uncharacteristically angry. "Han,
how gullible do you think the rest of the universe is?
You always want to do the right things for the wrong
reasons. Well, what will you do the day you run out of
excuses, son?"

Han pretended not to hear. "We'll punch through a
distress call just before we make our jump out of this
system. There'll be a Tion Hegemony gunboat here
before you know it. Come on, Chewie; let's break out
the handtruck and get the ship loaded before anything
else happens."

"Captain," Skynx called. Han paused and looked
back. "Here's a funny thing: I still think this adventuring was basically just danger and hardship a long
way from home, but now that it's ended and we're
parting company, I find myself saddened."

"Look us up for a refresher course, any time,"
offered Han.

Skynx shook his head. "I have much to do here; all too soon I'll be called away by my blood, when it's time to go chrysalis, then live a brief season as a çhroma-wing. If you wish to see me then, Captain, come and look on Ruuria for the flyer whose wing markings are the same as my own banding. The chroma-wing won't recognize you, but perhaps some part of Skynx will."

Han nodded, finding no adequate way to say goodbye. Badure called, "Hey, Slick!" Han and his copilot looked to him and he laughed. "Thanks, boys."

"Forget it." Han dismissed the entire incident. He started off again with his sidekick, both of them moving with some pain due to their injuries. "After all, a Life-Debt's a Life-Debt, isn't it, *partner?*" .

On this last note, he poked a knuckle into his copilot's ribs. Chewbacca swung angrily but not too quickly. Han ducked and the Wookiee backed off. "Look," Han said, "that's it for missions of mercy, all right? We're smugglers; that's what we know and that's what we're good at and that's what we're sticking to!"

The Wookiee growled concurrence. The others, surrounded by the endless shelf stacks of Xim's treasure, heard the discussion echo back from the corridor. Han broke into Chewbacca's rumblings with, "When the *Falcon*'s repaired and this wing of mine's fixed, we're going to try another Kessel spice run."

The Wookiee croaked an irritated objection. Han insisted. "It's fast money and we won't have to look at any dirt! We'll get Jabba the Hut or somebody to back us for a cut. Listen, I've got this plan . . ."

Just as they were moving out of earshot, Chewbacca's protests stopped. He and Han Solo shared some joke that made both laugh slyly. Then they returned to their schemes.

"There," Badure declared to Hasti, Skynx, Bollux, and Blue Max, "go the *real* Survivors."

ABOUT THE AUTHOR

BRIAN DALEY was born in rural New Jersey in 1947 and still resides there in a village most noteworthy as the home of Edgar Snow. After a four-year enlistment in the Army and holding down the usual odd jobs (waiter, bartender, loading-dock worker), Mr. Daley enrolled in college, where he began his first novel. *The Doomfarers of Coramonde* was published in 1977; its sequel, *The Starfollowers of Coramonde,* in 1979.

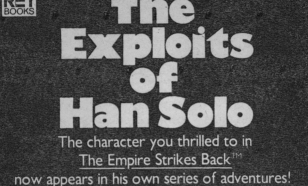